"Miss Maynard."
The man's voice was arresting

With an effort Christy dragged herself back to reality. "Good afternoon, Mr.—?"

"Sutcliffe. Brand Sutcliffe."

She realized with a shock that this was the man who had dragged her out here. "It was very good of you to meet me, Mr. Sutcliffe, but it wasn't really necessary. I could have taken a taxi."

The compelling voice was laced with acid. "Looking like that you'd have had to wait for some time. You look like you'd be more likely to ask for a tip than give one."

Christy gasped at his rudeness. "It was a sixteen-hour flight..." she started.

"And that tracksuit was a mess before you even arrived at the airport. What is it, ten years old? If it were a dog, I'd suggest you put it to sleep."

ELEANOR REES lives on the very edge of a little Chilterns town with a man who is the model for all her heroes—or so she tells him—and two cats. The cats, she says, approve of her writing as it keeps her lap stationary for long periods of time. Plus, the cats make their own contribution by strolling up and down the computer keyboard when Eleanor isn't looking. Her ambition is to write full-time and to live in the sort of place that gets snowbound in the winter. "I can't think of anything more romantic," she says.

Books by Eleanor Rees

HARLEQUIN PRESENTS
1285—THE SEAL WIFE

ELEANOR REES

pirate's hostage

Harlequin Books

TORONTO • NEW YORK • LONDON
AMSTERDAM • PARIS • SYDNEY • HAMBURG
STOCKHOLM • ATHENS • TOKYO • MILAN
MADRID • WARSAW • BUDAPEST • AUCKLAND

Harlequin Presents first edition April 1992
ISBN 0-373-11452-4

Original hardcover edition published in 1991
by Mills & Boon Limited

PIRATE'S HOSTAGE

CHAPTER ONE

'Miss. . .' The Chinese official looked down at the clipboard he carried. 'Miss Christabel Maynard—for Mr Brand Sutcliffe? Number one computer expert of London?'

Christy nodded, too tired even to raise a smile at his extravagant description, praying that whatever the query was would not cause too much delay. Already, she could see the queues building up at Passport Control as her fellow travellers streamed past her stationary luggage trolley. Even her resentment against the man whose sudden decision to buy a computer system from an obscure—though rapidly growing—English software house had dragged her halfway round the world at less than a day's notice was submerged in her overwhelming tiredness.

Christy glanced at her watch, mentally adding in the seven-hour time difference between London and Hong Kong. Thank goodness she was arriving at the end of the working day. Whatever his impatience, Mr Sutcliffe's unreasonable demands would have to wait until morning. And by then she might feel better able to cope.

But right now, all she wanted was to escape the crowds and go somewhere where she could sleep undisturbed by engine noises and 'turbulence' and the unsettling proximity of so many sleeping strangers. Somewhere she could try and come to terms with the changes that had so brutally usurped her life in the last forty-eight hours. A haven where at last she could let go and grieve for Sam. . .

'Please follow this way, Miss Maynard.' The official raised his arm and shouted something incomprehensible. Almost instantly, as if by some magical process, a wizened-looking porter appeared and took charge of her trolley, wheeling it off in the opposite direction to the stream of passengers with surprising energy for such a frail-looking frame.

With a yelp of surprise, Christy managed to retrieve her handbag before the trolley with her single suitcase disappeared from view in the crowd. Tucking it securely under her arm, she hurried after her guide, anxiety starting to twist a hard knot under her ribcage. Perhaps there was something wrong with her booking? It had all been done in such a rush. . .

'Is there a problem?' What if he didn't speak enough English to explain? All the signs she had seen so far were reassuringly bilingual, but, in a way, that only emphasised the absolute nature of the language barrier. The stylised characters of the Chinese translation didn't even look like words. 'Where are you taking me? Will it take long?'

'No problem.' They came to a rope barrier which her companion pushed aside and beckoned her through. 'No waitings here. Much better.' He gave an odd little half-bow, fingertips touching. 'For number one computer expert of London is no waitings. Please—over here.'

Following his gesture, Christy saw another row of Passport Control desks. There was no queue. For a moment, her heart rose—only to sink again when she noticed the bright yellow sign that hung above her waiting trolley. 'Hong Kong Residents Only'. . .

'Look!' She grabbed the official's arm and pointed desperately. 'It's no good—I'm not a Hong Kong resident.' She tried to pull back beyond the rope barrier. 'English—I'm English. From London.' Somehow she had been confused with someone else. With the 'number one computer expert', presumably.

'No problem. Passport, please.' Christy scrabbled in her handbag and pulled out her neat folder of documentation. Surely that would convince him.

'Look—British. I'm not a Hong Kong resident. I have to queue over there——' But guide and passport had already moved off towards the desk and she had no choice but to tag along behind them.

She watched in agony as the man behind the high counter flipped quickly through the pages, but the expected rejection didn't come. Instead, she was ushered through to where a bored-looking Customs official was waiting.

'Nothing to declare.' Her guide butted in before she could speak. The porter moved forward and to Christy's somewhat dazed amazement she was through. Only a few yards away, her fellow passengers were jostling for position as the queue moved slowly forwards. Whatever the mistake had been, it had certainly worked in her favour. It was less than five minutes since she had picked up her baggage.

* * *

'Good God!' The note of disparagement in the voice snapped her back to attention, and Christy swung round, her chin lifting in defiance. But the speaker had already turned to her guide, and was talking with apparent ease in what she assumed was Chinese. She was presented with nothing but the sight of his broad, unwelcoming back.

Tall even for a European, the man who had come to meet her seemed to tower over the mainly Chinese crowd like a giant among pygmies. The jacket of his dark suit was slung carelessly over one broad shoulder like a cloak, giving him a dangerously buccaneering look.

Christy felt a shiver of apprehension. Hong Kong was a very different world from the one she had left behind. A fiercer, less kindly world. And she knew instinctively that this man was a true denizen of it. . .

There was a discreet rustle of banknotes and the official bowed an obsequious farewell.

'Miss Maynard.' The man's voice had an arresting quality; it was a voice that would always make itself heard, Christy thought bemusedly. Through the noise of a crowded party—or the roar of a gale at sea. . .

With an effort, she dragged herself back to reality. 'Good afternoon, Mr, er——'

'Sutcliffe—Brand Sutcliffe.'

She realised with a start that this was the man who had dragged her out here; not just a buccaneer but the pirate captain himself. Despite the sheer unlikelihood of the head of a major Hong Kong trading company's turning out to meet her from the airport, the revelation didn't come as a surprise. There was an unmistakable air of leadership about him, in the way he stood and the way he held his head. . . The casual arrogance of command that came from long hours at the helm. . .

'Miss Maynard, are you all right?'

Flustered and embarrassed, Christy realised that her imagination was running away with her. No wonder he was looking at her with such disdain. 'Yes, yes—I'm sorry,' she stammered. 'I'm rather tired, that's all.'

Where on earth had she got this pirate image from? Sutcliffe's had some shipping interests—most of the big Hong Kong companies did, Mike had said—but this man was just another executive.

And yet. . .there was something about the relaxed way he held his long limbs that gave the lie to that; something in his overwhelmingly physical presence that suggested that the plush carpeting of an executive office was far from being his natural habitat.

'It was very good of you to meet me, Mr Sutcliffe, but it wasn't really necessary.' Under his critical gaze, she felt self-consciously aware that the old grey tracksuit she had worn for the flight, though comfortable, was neither elegant nor flattering, and that the sketchy *toilette* she had been able to make before landing did nothing to disguise the fact that she had slept badly, and in her clothes. 'I could have got a taxi.'

The compelling voice was tipped with acid. 'Looking like that, you'd have had to wait some time. You look more likely to ask for a tip than give one.'

Christy gasped at his rudeness. 'It was a sixteen-hour flight——' she started.

'And that tracksuit was a mess before you even arrived at the airport. What is it; ten years old? If it were a dog, I'd suggest you put it to sleep.' His eyes swept dismissively over the single case on the trolley. 'Is that all you've brought?'

'I hardly had much time for packing. And besides, I prefer to travel light.'

'"Light" is one thing—ill-equipped is something else. I take it you didn't intend to turn up in my office dressed like that?'

'I——'

Brand Sutcliffe looked at Christy enquiringly as she searched for a suitable retort, but none came. What was it about this infuriating man that seemed to paralyse her mental processes?

'Naturally, I have brought suitable working clothes, if that's what you mean,' she said lamely at last. 'Although I really don't see what business it is of yours what I wear, Mr Sutcliffe, so long as I do my job.'

'Don't you?' His voice was icy. 'This isn't cosy old England now, Miss Maynard. This is Hong Kong—and image is very important. I did try to explain to your partner. . .'

Breaking off as if in disgust, Brand turned and beckoned to the porter, speaking quickly in the strange, sing-song language she had heard him use earlier.

'Oh, well, I suppose we can sort you out. Come on—the car's outside. The sooner we get started, the better.' He gestured impatiently for her to follow as her luggage disappeared yet again into the crowds. 'And for God's sake stop looking so miserable. It can't be every day you get flown out to Hong Kong at someone else's expense. Who knows? You might actually enjoy it.'

Her powers of resistance completely exhausted, Christy tagged meekly behind her new guide as he led the way out of the concourse. But the moment she stepped out of the air-conditioned coolness of the terminal interior Christy knew he was wrong. She would never enjoy this place. Never.

It was the heat that hit her first, the humidity swamping her like a clogging blanket. And with the heavy air came the smell; not strong but curiously pervasive. A damp, dark brown, slightly sickly smell.

It was totally alien; totally foreign; like nothing she had ever smelt before.

The smell of Hong Kong, she thought fancifully. And wrinkled her nose in disgust.

The journey that followed did nothing to dispel Christy's initial impressions. Even the car's silken suspension—trust Sutcliffe to have something as ostentatious as a Rolls-Royce, she thought in irritation—couldn't disguise the bad state of the roads. And, looking out of the tinted windows, Christy could see that many of the buildings were in a similar state of disrepair.

Decrepit tenements rose drunkenly next to gleaming modern skyscrapers; bamboo scaffolding crawled up the walls of concrete office blocks; great empty gaps, like missing teeth, appeared where buildings had been demolished—or fallen down of their own accord. Roadworks blocked street after street, and slowed the rush-hour traffic to a horn-blaring crawl.

'Is it always like this?' He didn't even seem impatient, she thought crossly, as the stolid Chinese chauffeur's sudden dart for a gap in the next lane threw her heavily against Sutcliffe's shoulder.

'Like what? The traffic?' He sounded faintly surprised, as if noticing it for the first time. 'It's always pretty bad. The problem is, the city is split in two by the harbour, so the tunnel is inevitably a bottleneck. That's what we're queuing for now. The airport is in Kowloon—on the mainland. So are my offices, but I live on Hong Kong island and that's where I've booked your hotel.'

'Wouldn't it have saved time to choose a hotel on the mainland side?' Christy could hear the irritation in her own voice. She was so tired. . . 'I can't go through this every day.'

'Don't worry, no one's asking you to. Normally I cross by ferry. But I was expecting you to have brought rather more luggage—and this way I can show you something of the city.'

'I've already seen quite enough, thank you.' At last they were in the tunnel. 'This isn't a sightseeing trip.'

'And it doesn't have to be a martyrdom, either,' he pointed out mildly. 'I appreciate your coming out at such short notice—and I don't expect you to keep your nose to the grindstone twenty-four hours a day, seven days a week. I thought at the weekend I could show you——'

'Please don't bother, Mr Sutcliffe. I've seen enough to know that Hong Kong isn't somewhere I'd visit for pleasure.'

'In twenty minutes? From the window of a car?' He started to say something else, then stopped as the car emerged into the light again, horn blaring almost immediately as it jostled for position. They lapsed into a silence that was anything but companionable.

The big car stopped and started its way through the crowded streets, the tall buildings on either side festooned with brightly coloured signs advertising everything from topless nightcubs to jade carving.

Christy stared fixedly out of the window, her awareness of the man beside her like a fire in her skin. She should never have let Mike persuade her to come to this alien place. Only, with his new wife's pregnancy having been confirmed on the very morning that Sutcliffe had phoned with his urgent commission, her normally mild boss had been unexpectedly firm.

'It's got to be you, Christy,' he'd said bluntly. 'You're my partner, near as dammit, and it's about time you accepted that and started sharing the responsibilities. I can't leave Carol now, you must see that.'

Well, it was too late now. She had let him talk her into it—and it was clear that she had made a terrible mistake.

Unfortunately it came as no comfort to reflect that Brand Sutcliffe was almost certainly thinking the same.

She glanced at him surreptitiously and realised with chagrin that his eyes were closed. He wasn't even aware of her. . . And then she noticed something that hadn't caught her attention before. A scar, about two inches long, white against the tanned skin of his face. Just below the right eye. It must have registered subconsciously—no wonder she had seen him as a pirate.

Christy shivered, suddenly very aware of how alone she was in this alien landscape. It was ridiculous, of course. He was just a businessman. Probably he'd got the scar by walking into a filing cabinet. So why did she feel so strong a presentiment of danger?

'Look, Mr Sutcliffe, I appreciate your help, but I'd rather do my unpacking myself. And to be honest, all I want to do at the moment is fall into bed. So if you don't mind. . .'

'Ah, but I do. And call me Brand. It seems a little formal to be calling me "Mr Sutcliffe" when I'm sorting through your frillies.' He smiled, and Christy thought that she had never met a man before who could combine such charm with such a devastating disregard for the normal social courtesies. 'What do I call you? Christabel?'

Only her father ever called her Christabel—and then only when he was trying to persuade her to buy into one of his crazy 'sure-fire' schemes. Like the other night. . .

But she didn't want to think about that. That had been the first shock of the earthquake that had brought her life tumbling about her, although Mike's

marriage a few months earlier had started the warning tremors.

'I prefer Christy,' she said shortly. 'Brand, I
think——'

But she wasn't allowed to finish. 'Sleeping is the
last thing you should do right now,' her infuriating
companion pointed out. 'It's only teatime here,
remember. If I let you sleep, you'd be wide awake by
three in the morning and it would take you days to
adjust. Believe me, it's better to stick it out.'

He emptied the contents of her suitcase on to the
bed and started to pick them over. 'What the hell's
this?'

'It's my nightdress.' She snatched the full cotton
garment from his hands and started to re-fold it. 'As
you can see, I don't wear "frillies". Brand, will you
please leave my things alone?'

'I'm only trying to help,' he said soothingly. 'And
besides, I have to establish the extent of the damage.'
He looked down at the tangled pile with an
expression of distaste. 'Didn't your partner tell you
anything about the position here?' he went on
brusquely. 'These clothes might be adequate for a
brief holiday in Bournemouth, but they're hardly
suitable for a high-profile job like this one. And as
for this suit. . . What is it, your old school uniform?'

Guiltily, Christy remembered Mike's urging that
she spend a morning shopping before catching the
plane—and his unprecedented suggestion that the
firm would pay for it. 'I—he did say something, but
I didn't really have anything suitable,' she said

defensively. 'And I thought I could buy some stuff here.'

For the first time, Brand looked at her with a hint of approval. 'Well, that's sensible enough,' he agreed. 'Hong Kong is a clothes-shopper's paradise. But what did you expect to wear in the meantime? I didn't fly you out here so that you could spend the first week browsing round the shops. I realise you'll be tired, but I want to make a start first thing tomorrow.'

'Well, I thought my suit——' But the look on her face stopped her. 'Well, what would you suggest, then, since you're so fussy?'

'I'd suggest you leave it to me.' He walked over to the phone and started to dial. 'And in future, if I give you instructions, I suggest you follow them. Next time it may be more difficult to sort things out.'

There was a pause while Christy began to tidy the clothes on the bed. Angry though Brand's attitude made her, it was impossible now not to see her possessions through his censorious eyes. They did look old. . . How had she never noticed how drab that suit looked? He was right—there was nothing there which was right for the job she had come here to do.

'Hello, Rainbow?' The unlikely name caught Christy's attention, although she hadn't intended to eavesdrop. 'Look, Miss Maynard has arrived from London—yes, that's right; the computer expert. Only most of her baggage seems to have gone astray. Could you get some stuff sent over—just enough for a couple of days? No, you'd better assume she's lost everything—she'll need a suit and all the trimmings. Have it put on my account.'

He paused, then turned to look at Christy. 'She's— oh, about five feet four, I'd say. Slim build.' He covered the mouthpiece with his hand. 'What size are you, Christy?'

'About a ten.'

'English size ten—that'll be a six, I think. Blonde hair.' Christy flushed. Was he teasing her? Her hair was hardly blonde. . . More like mouse, except for a few weeks in summer when it caught the sun. 'Pale skin. Grey-blue eyes.' Brand laughed at some comment that Christy couldn't hear. 'You're right, she is. Only I don't think she knows it. Thanks a lot, Rainbow; I knew I could count on you.' Still smiling, he put down the phone.

The suspicion that he was mocking her made Christy snappish. 'Why didn't you tell her the truth—that I just hadn't brought the right things? I haven't lost my cases.'

His smile vanished. 'Because you'd have lost face.' Chrisy raised her eyebrows in disbelief and Brand frowned. 'It's no joke out here, Christy—it's deadly serious. "Face"—image, prestige or whatever you want to call it—is vitally important.'

'But surely it hardly matters about my prestige?' It all seemed so ridiculous; like something from a historical novel. 'I'll be back in England in a couple of weeks.'

'You'll be back there a damn sight sooner than that if you don't make some attempt to understand what I'm trying to say.' There was an undercurrent of anger in his voice which stifled her amusement. 'You've already messed up turning up at the airport looking like a badly wrapped parcel. I'm going to spell this out for you, Christy—and you'd better listen. Why do you think I'm buying this system in the first place?'

She stared at him blankly. 'Well, because you need it, I suppose. To run your business more efficiently.'

'That's true—but it's only part of it. And the rest is face. If all I wanted was a new computer, I could have bought one locally. But if buying a new system is good face, then flying to England to buy one is even better.'

He looked at her intently, as if trying to see if his words were sinking in. 'Christy, face is something I need badly at the moment. I have some very delicate negotiations in progress and the slightest thing could tip the balance. Like having my "number one computer expert" turning up dressed like a refugee from St Trinian's.'

'So that was you, was it—all this "expert" stuff? What are you trying to pull, Brand? I came here to do a technical job of work—not to be used in some kind of juvenile publicity stunt.'

'I'm not trying to "pull" anything.' He was speaking now with exaggerated slowness and clarity, as if explaining to a slightly retarded child. 'It's just the way things are done over here. Think of all those shop signs we passed driving back from the airport, Christy. Remember the names? "Excellent Food Emporium", "Top-Class Fabrics—"Number One" this, "Worldwide" that. They aren't meant as a joke.

Extravagance is the norm here; it's what people expect. Sell yourself short and you'll get nowhere.'

Her lack of conviction must have been evident. He shook his head in frustration. 'Well, believe me, I've done you a favour. You'll get a much better hearing now because people will be predisposed to give you respect. All you have to do now is prove that you can earn it.'

'So that you can pull off your precious "negotiations"?'

'Don't be childish. It isn't just me who benefits. Hong Kong is notoriously fashion-conscious—and not just in clothes. If your systems became fashionable, you could find yourselves overrun with orders. But it means some hard work from you. You've got to knock them dead.'

He smiled down at her, his eyes suddenly softened. 'Don't look so scared, Christy. Lecture's over. You can do it—with a little bit of help from your friends.'

But his kindness seemed to be the final straw. Her father's pleading, Sam's death, and Mike's callous insistence on sending her on this trip all seemed to mingle with the strain of the journey and the humiliation of having her wardrobe treated so dismissively.

To her horror, Christy felt something inside her crack. Her control finally shattered, and she felt the sensible Christy—the one who could cope, the one who never let go—step aside.

'I can't!' she heard some quite different Christy wail. 'I'm not that sort of person—I can't do that sort of thing. I came here to do a job—a technical job. Why can't you just leave me alone?'

'Because you're all I've got.' Brand Sutcliffe's voice was soft but implacable in her ears. 'I need a system, and I need it fast—and it's too late to think of finding another company to provide it now. You'll just have to grin and bear it. I need you. And I intend to make sure that you don't let me down.'

'But it's just not fair!' Christy knew she sounded like a spoilt child, but somehow she couldn't stop. Less than three days ago she had been perfectly content. Sam had been alive; she had had her routine and she had been happy. But now that ordered existence seemed like a faraway dream.

'Everything's going wrong!' And to complete her humiliation she burst into tears.

But she was too tired to feel ashamed. She sank down on the clothes-strewn bed, mopping her eyes with the first thing that came to hand.

'What kind of everything?' Brand sat down beside her and touched her gently under the chin, turning her head so that she was looking into his eyes.

But she shook her head away. 'It's all your fault,' she heard herself sob incoherently. 'Yours and Mike's. . . I was happy before—maybe it was boring, but I didn't think so. And I had Sam. . . But then he got killed, and it all started going wrong. And I was pleased about the baby, but it was his idea to advertise abroad and he said I wouldn't have to do any travelling. And I couldn't afford to lend him any money and even if I could, I wouldn't. But I feel so guilty. . . Why can't people leave me alone?'

Brand was staring at her as if she was talking gibberish. 'I thought people who worked with computers were supposed to be logical?' he said at last. But there was a new gentleness in his voice. 'Who was Sam, Christy? Your partner didn't say anything about that.'

'That's because he doesn't care.' The sensible Christy looked on helplessly as the tears started to flow afresh. 'He called him "that cat" and pretended to be sorry, but really he was glad because it meant he could send me on this trip. But I'd had him ever since I left home, and I loved him——'

'Sam was a cat? And he's dead?' He sounded almost pleased, she thought belligerently. 'So presumably he wasn't the father of the baby?'

'I don't know what you're talking about.' Christy felt her sensible self slip back into place as she stared at him in puzzlement.

'Then the confusion is mutual. For a moment there, I thought you were telling me that your lover had died, leaving you pregnant and feeling guilty because you'd refused to lend him money. Then I find out that your lover is actually a cat—it makes the rest of the scenario seem rather less likely. Could you run it past me again?'

'It's nothing.' She could feel her face burning as she realised how completely she had given herself away. How could she have lost control like that? 'It doesn't matter,' she muttered, hastily scrubbing at her eyes as if she could wipe out the humiliation she was feeling.

'Oh, yes, it does.' The gentleness was still there.

'If for no other reason that it would stop me dying of curiosity trying to work it out. But more importantly, I'd say you needed to talk. From the way it came gushing out just then, you must have been bottling it up for quite a time.'

'Well, there's not really anyone to talk to.' Christy was appalled by the desolation she heard in her own words. Since when had she ever been lonely? A loner, yes—but hadn't that seemed the best way? She had learned to depend on her own resources, living with a father who was more worried about his latest business scheme than where the next meal was coming from. At least then no one could let you down. . .

'I used to talk to Mike, but since he got married. . . I like Carol, and of course I'm pleased for them, but it's not the same. And it sounds stupid, but I used to talk to Sam——'

'Then talk to me. If it will help, I'll lie on your lap and purr.' Before she could react, he had twisted round and lay with his head in her lap, beaming up at her with a smile of such beatific innocence that it was impossible not to respond. 'That's better. Now tell Uncle Brand.'

She could feel his voice rumbling through the back of his neck into her legs; into her bones. A deep, reassuring sound—not unlike Sam's comforting purr. It was a ridiculous situation, but she was too tired and disorientated to care. She had to stifle an urge to stroke the dark waves of hair which framed his face.

And somehow telling him seemed easy; easier than

forcing the lid back on the box of her memories. 'There's not much to tell. I'm being silly really—I suppose nothing stays the same. But since Sam got run over, I keep thinking, if only I hadn't let him out. . . He never normally went out much, you see. He was a house-cat; not streetwise at all. Usually I watched him all the time, but I was upset. . .'

Upset because her father had been round yet again. Upset because no matter how many times she turned him down, it always left the sour taste of guilt in her mouth.

Brand's eyes were closed, his lashes unexpectedly long and dark against his cheek. Almost touching that pale scar. . . And he listened; not like Mike, impatiently, but as if he understood. As if it wasn't foolish to mourn for a cat.

'He was killed the day you phoned about this job. I still can't believe—he meant such a lot to me, you see.'

She broke off to gulp back the tears. 'But it wasn't just Sam dying,' she went on more controlledly. 'It's just that everything seems to be changing at once. Mike got married a couple of months ago—and now they're having a baby. That's why I had to come instead of him. And I hate travelling; I hate all this change and disturbance. I'm not the sort of person you need, Brand. I'll only mess it up. If only Mike had come himself——'

She felt her eyes start to fill again, and pushed ineffectually at the weight of his head on her lap. 'Get up, Brand. This is stupid.'

'It's not stupid.' He hauled himself up to sit beside

her and gently touched her cheek. 'And you're not going to mess it up. Don't underestimate yourself— you're not a natural coward, Christy. There's a fighter inside you, but until you stop running you'll never know your strength. Treat it as a game—and pretend I'm your coach. All you have to do is listen when I'm explaining the rules.'

She managed a watery smile. 'Which are?'

'There's really only one. Brazen it out.' His eyes gleamed mischievously. And if you're going to blow your nose on your knickers in public, make sure they're Janet Reger rather than tatty chainstore. Face, remember?'

She looked down, startled, at the crumpled ball of fabric in her hand. And started to laugh.

CHAPTER TWO

IT WAS a few hours later, in the hotel restaurant, and Brand Sutcliffe was looking at her across the table. Christy could feel her skin prickle as his gaze stroked her, tracing the curves of her body under the floral cotton of her dress.

But that was fantasy. This was a business dinner—nothing more. She was explaining the details of the service MW Systems could provide, as she had for dozens of customers before. It was ridiculous to feel so. . .naked. So exposed. Only——

Only what? Only she had never tried to sell a computer system to a pirate before? Never explained the difference between hardware and software to a man who lounged back in his seat with quite that attitude of casual arrogance? Somehow he made her feel as if he were a buyer at some Eastern slave-market and it was her own charms she was selling.

But she was letting her imagination run away with her. With an effort of will, Christy dragged her attention back to the work she had come here to do.

'Buying a computer system is like buying a suit,' she explained carefully. 'If you buy off the peg, you can walk out of the shop with it there and then—and if you're lucky it will more or less fit you.'

Involuntarily, her eye took in the dark cloth which moulded itself so sleekly to his broad shoulders. No mass production could have achieved such flawless lines. 'But if you want something tailor-made, you have to wait a lot longer and pay a lot more. What we do is provide a compromise. You buy the system off the peg, but the price includes the services of a "tailor" who will come and adjust it until it does just what you want it to do.'

'So what happens? Do you come and take my inside-leg measurement?'

He was deliberately teasing her. Well, she wouldn't give him the satisfaction of rising to his bait. 'Something like that,' she said blandly. 'We can install the basic system immediately; that's what gives us a chance of meeting your deadlines. But while I'm out here, I'll also be beginning the analysis to find out what you *really* need. I'll have to spend a week or so studying your operation and asking questions. But that's the beauty of our customisation plan. It lets you have your cake and eat it.'

'It sounds. . .tempting.' How did he manage to fit so much seductive warmth into one little word? The man ought to carry a government health warning. 'But you are quite certain that you can do it? You do realise that I need this system urgently? By nine forty-three p.m. on Saturday, October the seventh, to be exact.'

So Mike hadn't exaggerated about the tight time-scales. October was only four weeks away. 'I'm sure we can do it if we have to,' she said carefully. 'And if the equipment is delivered on time. But why on earth. . .?'

'Why the precise schedule?'

Brand leaned forwards and reached out a hand across the table. Christy started back; then cursed herself for letting him rattle her when all he did was pick a clover-shaped roll from the basket between them.

'Because I'm planning to re-launch Sutcliffe's in a big way, complete, I hope, with a new computer system. And the local *Fung Shui* expert has decreed that that is the most auspicious date and time this century for new beginnings.' He sounded completely serious, and Christy looked at him askance. Was he pulling her leg?

'What——'

'And before you ask what *Fung Shui* is,' he went on resignedly, 'it's a kind of earth magic—the Chinese way of making sure you live in harmony with your surroundings.'

Christy could feel her jaw drop. 'You mean you want me to knock myself out to deliver a system in a month because some Chinese fortune-teller picked some numbers out of a hat? You can't be serious.' But his face didn't change.

'I assure you I can. In Hong Kong, *Fung Shui* is no joking matter. Not for anyone who wants to stay in business.'

'But you can't believe. . .'

'Can't I?' His tone was lightly mocking, daring her to disagree. 'But in any case, that's irrelevant. My workforce, my customers and most importantly my backers do believe it—that's what's important. Now, can you meet that deadline or not?'

She would not let him fluster her. 'I've already

explained that we can—although, naturally, we can't be responsible for the hardware. But living in Hong Kong there shouldn't be much difficulty with that. I've got the contract here somewhere. . .' She reached down to the briefcase by her chair, but his hand caught hers and held it prisoner on the linen tablecloth.

'Don't bother, Christy. I'll sign it tomorrow. We've talked enough business for one evening.' His palm was hard and callused against her skin. Not a businessman's hand at all.

'Are you sure you don't have any more questions?'

'Not about the system. What a single-minded young woman you are, Christy.' Her name sounded like a caress and Christy felt his fingers tighten on hers. He was still holding her hand! Mortified, she snatched it away and saw his face twitch in amusement as the blood rushed to her cheeks.

'It's you I find interesting, Christy.' He was looking at her again, his eyes closing the distance between them until they were the only two people in the restaurant. 'It was very good of you to fly out at such short notice. I hope it hasn't caused you too many problems.'

'Nothing I can't cope with.' And in fact, she was beginning to realise that a break with routine might be just what she needed. It would keep her out of her father's way and give her time to recover from Sam's loss without constant reminders. Deprived of the old cat's comforting presence, the familiar rooms of her flat had seemed cold and impersonal. No longer a home. . .

But Brand was determined not to be choked off. He raised his eyebrows. 'I find that difficult to believe. No jealous boyfriend gnashing his teeth?'

'I told you; I don't have any commitments.' He was fishing, but she had no intention of being caught. Men like Brand Sutcliffe were trouble; and, if there was one skill which Christy had perfected, it was the art of staying out of trouble. She had already let him far further into her private life than she had had any intention of allowing.

But his persistence unsettled her and she could feel her heart beating faster. She felt. . .hunted. And there was a disturbingly unexpected element in her response. A desire to be caught. . .

If only he would stop looking at her like that. As if this were a meeting between two lovers instead of a business lunch. As if he was wondering where it would end.

To her relief, she saw a little fat waiter weaving his way between the tables towards them. 'Are you ready to order?'

'Oh, I think so.' He grinned. 'I always know what I want. It's getting it that's sometimes the problem.'

Christy was suddenly assailed by an image of him climbing the side of a ship, a knife clenched between those strong white teeth. Stand by to repel boarders. . .

'If it's on the menu, then surely they'll have it?' Only somehow she got the feeling he wasn't talking about the food.

* * *

'Prawn cocktail?'

The two men spoke almost in chorus, Brand in a tone of accusation and the waiter in one of delicately concealed disgust.

'Yes, prawn cocktail.' Stubbornly, Christy stuck to her guns, determined not to be intimidated by the expensive elaboration of the menu. 'I know it's not down here, but you've got prawns in garlic butter on the menu, so you must have prawns. And I'm sure your chef can manage some seafood dressing, can't he?'

'Er. . .yes, madam. Prawn cocktail.' The waiter made it sound as if she had asked for a live snake—although judging from some of the selections in the Chinese section of the menu, Christy thought with a shudder, that might have been more to his taste. She had read as far as the 'cold braised jellyfish' before hastily turning the page.

'And to follow?' The little man hovered over her anxiously. 'Can I recommend the——?'

'I'll just have a well-done steak, please. With nothing on it. No sauce or anything. And can you please make sure that it's very well-done?' she added firmly, as he wrote down the order with a pained expession on his face. 'I don't like it to be pink at all.'

'Very well, madam.' He turned to Brand as if in supplication. 'And for you, Mr Sutcliffe? We have some very good oysters this evening, sir. Chef asked me to mention them. . .'

'Thanks. I'll have a dozen, then, and the Tournedos Rossini—rare, please. And to drink. . .' He ran an obviously practised eye down the wine-list and made a couple of selections that left the waiter beaming with obsequious pleasure.

'Certainly, sir. I'll tell the *sommelier*.'

Leaning back in his chair, Brand watched the man move away, then turned an accusing eye on his companion.

'You do realise,' he said, with a mildness that made Christy's neck prickle, 'that this hotel has one of the best chefs in Hong Kong?'

'Then he probably knows how to make a prawn cocktail,' she retorted. Attack was the only line of defence with a man like Brand. 'I'm just not very keen on foreign food.'

'Isn't that rather a sweeping statement?' He raised his eyebrows with a air of superiority that Christy found almost insufferable. 'You'll be missing out on a lot in Hong Kong if you don't take advantage of its restaurants, you know. It's not just Chinese— although that's superb, of course. There's just about every nationality in the world here, from Dutch to Vietnamese. Are you telling me you *always* have prawn cocktail when you eat out? Don't you ever feel the urge to experiment?'

'I'm not really the experimental type.' She would not let him push her into an argument. 'I've never seen the point of ordering something I probably won't like just because it's different. If I have prawn cocktail I know I'll enjoy it, so why take the risk? What's wrong with prawn cocktail, anyway?'

'Nothing's wrong with it—just as there's nothing wrong with that. . .outfit.' The blandness of his tone almost disguised the insult, but his half-smile and the way his eyes flickered disparagingly over her dress left no room for doubt. 'Except that both are boring, cowardly and totally lacking in imagination.'

He was deliberately baiting her. Despite her resolution to stay calm, Christy felt her temper beginning to rise. 'There is nothing wrong with the way I dress——' she started.

'Oh, nothing at all,' he agreed with disarming speed. 'And there's nothing wrong with living on a diet of prawn cocktail and burnt steak—or with investing all your emotional energies in a married man and a dead cat. But it does start to say something about your character, wouldn't you say?'

'I—oh! How dare you?' More than ever, Christy found herself regretting the confidences she had so stupidly shared with this unfeeling pig of a man. 'I never—Mike and I never——'

'No, I don't suppose you did. And I expect that suited you very well. No risks; no excitements. . .' Christy just stared at him, speechless, as he went on musingly, 'I'm beginning to think I ought to take you in hand. Something tells me, Miss Maynard, that what you need is a crash course in living dangerously.'

'And you'd make the ideal teacher, I suppose?' Sarcasm seemed a safer way of relieving her feelings than outright anger. Tempting though it was to tell this infuriatingly self-confident man exactly what she thought of him, the knowledge that he was still, after all, a client held her back from the brink. 'I suppose that's how you got that scar under your eye, is it? "Living dangerously"?'

As soon as the words were out, she froze. What if he was sensitive about the injury? But he didn't seem to be annoyed; more amused. His fingers went up to touch the silvery scar-tissue, as if he had forgotten it was there.

'Changing the subject?' he murmured. 'What are you afraid of, I wonder? Very well, Christy, I will allow you to turn the tables. Perhaps you will "love me for the dangers I have passed".'

Christy recognised the allusion and blushed. If Brand Sutcliffe thought she was going to play Desdemona to his Othello, he was very much mistaken. If he had known her a little better, he would have realised that she was the last person to be impressed by tales of an adventurous lifestyle. Life with Poppa and his endless 'schemes' had cured her of that for ever.

But she said nothing. In her experience, the best way to keep men from asking awkward questions was to allow them to talk at tedious length about themselves.

'This, I'm afraid, was a relic of my own stupidity.' Brand touched the scar again, tracing the line of it with his finger in a way that Christy found very disturbing. What would it feel like, that silvery skin? 'I got it in the China Seas race about five years ago, when a spinnaker sheet parted.'

He grinned at her blank expression. 'You computerites aren't the only ones with a private language, you know. Sailors have been doing it for centuries.'

Christy found herself almost smiling back, her anger starting to dissolve in the warmth of his charm.

Perhaps she was being over-sensitive; he was probably just teasing her. It didn't mean anything. He was good company—she had almost forgotten her tiredness. And he's very attractive, a voice at the back of her mind added treacherously. She felt herself blush. 'So are you going to translate for me?'

'It means that I was dense enough to try and use a sail in winds that were about a hundred per cent too strong for it—and the rope that was controlling it snapped. The loose end sprang back and knocked me for six, doing its best to leave me an eye short on the way. But luckily my guardian angel was on duty at the time, and I only lost the race.'

He stared down at his plate, his face suddenly serious. 'Although at the time it didn't seem much of a bargain. I had a lot riding on that race.'

'But nothing could be worse than losing an eye!'

'No? Well, with hindsight, I would agree with you, but at the time I'd have given almost anything to win. I had a bet on the race, you see. With my brother.'

'A bet?' Christy's voice was scornful. 'What on earth could you have bet that would have been worth——?'

'Everything.' He looked her straight in the eye, challenging her. 'Sutcliffe's. My home. My future. Everything.' There was a long silence while Christy tried to comprehend what he was telling her. 'And I lost.'

'I don't understand. . .' But already she was beginning to understand all too well. And the feeling of disappointment which Brand's confession kindled disturbed her by its intensity. Why should she care that a man she had met only hours before had turned out to be the type of irresponsible playboy who could lose a fortune on a whim?

'You gambled everything on some sort of race?'

'Well, not quite everything. My mother left me some money of my own, which wasn't included. And I kept the boat. But apart from that, yes, it stripped me pretty bare. And——' his voice was suddenly edged with bitterness '—well, let's just say, I lost some things I hadn't even realised I was risking. It was a bad time, all in all. An eye might have seemed like fair exchange.'

Christy just stared at him. Did he actually think he was going to enlist her sympathy? 'Well, it obviously didn't hold you back for long. You're hardly destitute.' It was childish to feel so. . .betrayed. Just because she had almost made up her mind to like him. 'What happened? Did you play him double or quits? Or did he just forget to collect?'

'Oh, no—he collected all right.' The bitterness was there again, though better camouflaged this time. 'My brother wasn't the forgetful type when it came to collecting what he was owed. Or anything else that was—on offer.'

'So let me guess.' Christy couldn't keep the sarcasm out of her voice. It was like listening to Poppa all over again. . . 'But this time it's going to be different, Christy. This one's a certainty. If I can just raise the initial investment. . .' 'I suppose you worked your way back up from nothing entirely by your own unaided efforts?'

Brand looked almost hurt. 'Now, why do I get the impression I have a hostile audience?'

'Because quite frankly, Mr Sutcliffe, I find it difficult to get excited about your little setbacks, particularly since they seem to be entirely your own fault.' Christy knew that she was being recklessly undiplomatic, but somehow she couldn't stop. 'Maybe I am conservative and boring, but anyone irresponsible enough to gamble away their livelihood gets no sympathy from me—and you don't even look as if you need it. You obviously recouped your lost fortunes, and since you're buying our computer system I'm quite prepared to listen to how you did it. But don't expect me to be impressed.'

'My God.' This time his voice was tight with anger. 'You really are something, aren't you? How often do you open that closed mind of yours? Once a year? Once a decade?'

Belatedly, Christy realised that she had gone too far. What if he decided to pull out? If she lost the sale. . . Oh, why hadn't Mike handled this? 'I'm sorry,' she said weakly. 'I shouldn't have said that; it was rude. It's just——'

But what could she say, without making things worse? That she knew men like him backwards, with their vanity and their eternal conviction that the universe would fall in with their plans? That she had spent seventeen years of her life veering from rags to riches and back again to rags, listening patiently to her father's exploits and excuses—and that life was too short to waste on replaying that same tape yet again?

'Just what, Christy?' Brand was looking at her with undisguised disdain. 'Just that I don't fit your petty ideas of respectability? Just that you'd like to pretend that the little circle of light you can see from your safe little burrow is the whole big sky?'

The contempt in his voice paralysed her. 'What are you afraid of, Christy? What caused the big freeze?' His eyes probed her ruthlessly, demanding her secrets. 'I was wrong about you—it's not just living dangerously you need lessons in. Somehow, you've never learned to live at all.'

It was too much. Inside, Christy could feel the storm of emotions beating against the fragile barrier of her self-control. Outside, her face and voice were icy calm.

'Enjoy your food, Mr Sutcliffe.' She pushed back the chair and stood up with exaggerated care, as if the least untoward movement might cause an explosion. 'I find I'm not very hungry after all—but please stay and finish your meal.'

Not that he looked like doing anything else, she thought bitterly as she made her way towards the exit. He made no attempt to restrain her—not even the slightest polite pretence of an apology. She would not look back. No doubt if she did he would be concentrating unconcernedly on his food——

But he wasn't. As a worried-looking waiter rushed to pull the door open, its glass surface formed for a split second an almost perfect mirror against the dark surface behind.

By some trick of the light, she could see him sitting

there, hands clenched, his gaze fixed on her retreating back. Just for that moment, their eyes met—and she was looking into his soul. It was on fire. And the feeling that burned there terrified her.

CHAPTER THREE

THE pirate was standing over her, his linen shirt loose to the waist and his breeches tight against the muscles of his thighs. 'You belong to me now—I bought you, at the market.' He looked down at her and started to flick the buttons from her grey suit with the tip of his sword. Christy stared back at him; half afraid and half—what? Half expectant. . .

It was true; Mike had sold her, she remembered. He had sold her to buy a baby for his wife. It wasn't his fault. . .

'Take off your clothes.' But she was already naked. She could feel his eyes on her, and then his hands. And then his lips——

Christy woke with a start, pushing back the covers and struggling to sit up. The touch of the sheets on her skin reminded her of her unaccustomed nakedness. The crumpled linen had left red weals on her soft, sleep-warmed flesh and for a moment she was back in the dream. The pirate. . .had it been true? Had he——?

Then the memories started to filter back. Of course; she had come back to the room to find that someone had packed away all the clothes she had left on the bed, and she had been too tired even to look for her nightdress. All her clothes would be so creased. She was back in the real world and the dream faded from her mind.

But Brand had been right yet again, she realised with irritation as she peered at the hands of her travelling clock. It was only six and she was awake already— unnaturally awake, considering the pall of tiredness which still hung over her jet-lagged brain.

If she had gone to bed earlier, she would probably have woken hours ago. But at least she wouldn't be late on her first morning. After their *contretemps* in the restaurant, it would be unwise to give him any ammunition at all.

She swung her legs over the side of the bed and stood up unsteadily, looking around the room which she had hardly noticed the night before. It was big, swallowing the king-size bed she had slept on with luxurious ease. There was a small sofa and easy-chair arranged around a low table under the window and almost one side of the room was taken up by fitted wardrobes, with mirrored doors.

As she stared at them, her naked self looked back at her, strangely unfamiliar. She turned away, uncomfortably. At home, the only full-length mirror was in the hallway and it would never have occurred to her to look at herself in the nude. . .

The curtains were open, and she wandered over to the window. Some twenty floors below her, tiny figures were swimming in the hotel pool while others sat around the edge at tables, eating. But they were all oblivious of the small drama she could see being played out from her vantage point.

She watched, fascinated, as the sinuous striped body of a cat edged nearer and nearer to one table, whose occupants were both in the pool. Leaving their breakfasts behind. A waiter bustled past, and the striped shadow froze—then restarted its single-minded stalking.

Then everything happened at once. A man pulled himself out of the pool and saw the cat. He dived towards it, shouting. The waiter ran back and collided with the man, dropping a pile of plates to shatter on the ground. And the cat, no doubt deciding that it was now or never, made a dive for the table and seized whatever breakfast delicacy it had had its eye on. Within seconds, it had vanished over the wall.

Christy smiled, and felt her heart lighten. Looking outwards, she realised that her initial impression of Hong Kong as a concrete jungle had been unfair. Behind the tall grey skyscrapers of the coastal strip, a mist hung over a backdrop of green hills. And to her right she could just see the sun sparkling off the waters of the harbour.

Although some things hadn't changed. Down below, the traffic was already starting its chorus. It was a strange, almost wanton sensation to be looking out, naked, on a whole city full of people.

Without thinking, she ran her hands down her body and felt her nipples tighten—then blushed as a flash of memory betrayed her. His hands on her breasts. . . The memory of a dream.

She shivered and pushed it away. Coping with Brand Sutcliffe was going to be difficult enough without letting her imagination play tricks on her. First a shower. And then she would have to see about ironing something to wear.

* * *

Christy's first thought when she slid back the wardrobe door was that she had woken up in someone else's room. These were certainly someone else's clothes.

Never in her life had she worn anything as brilliant as that peacock-blue suit in raw silk—or as impractical as the pure white crêpe de Chine T-shirt which hung next to it. And as for the lingerie—the pale blue satin camisole and french knickers were hardly her idea of sensible underwear. Could they have been left by the room's last occupant? And yet surely she would have seen them the evening before?

And then she remembered. Of course; these had to be the clothes the mysterious Rainbow had been charged with delivering. But somehow there had been a breakdown in communication. Christy wondered with a flush of embarrassment if the girl had believed she was shopping for Brand's mistress. None of these clothes were the least bit suitable for work.

She smiled with rather unkind satisfaction at the thought of all Brand's planning going to waste. It would have to be the grey suit after all. She laid out a towel on the desk-top to protect the wood and plugged in her portable iron. Then she opened her suitcase.

It was empty. And a brief frenzied search revealed that the room's drawers and cupboards were similarly void. It wasn't just a case of an over-zealous maid with a passion for tidying. It had to be Brand Sutcliffe. Quite how he had managed it, she wasn't certain.

But he had stolen her clothes.

'Ah, yes; Miss Maynard. I am Rainbow, Mr Sutcliffe's confidential assistant. Good morning.'

The Chinese girl rose gracefully from behind her desk and Christy held out her hand to shake, only to pull it back feeling foolish when the girl ignored it, giving instead a slight nodding bow. 'You are very welcome.' Was it just the difference in culture that made the greeting sound empty—or even hostile?

The girl's face gave nothing away, the smooth Oriental features like a beautiful painted mask. 'Mr Sutcliffe has been delayed for a few minutes. He asked me to look after you. Please follow me.'

She moved off down the corridor and Christy followed, feeling ridiculously ungainly in comparison with her guide's tiny figure. One heel caught in the deep pile of an obviously new carpet, and Christy cursed under her breath.

She never wore high heels normally, and the extra height added to her feeling of clumsiness. As if it wasn't bad enough being dressed up like something out of one of the more glitzy television soap-operas, without being forced to walk on what amounted to stilts. Thank goodness Brand had sent the Rolls for her again. At this rate, she'd never have made it to the ferry without breaking a leg.

'Mr Sutcliffe will be with you in a moment. Would you like a cup of coffee?' Once more, the words were friendly enough, but Christy was left with an impression of coldness that was difficult to explain. Feeling that she was probably being unfair—the Chinese were meant to be inscrutable after all—she accepted the offer with more than usual warmth and, when it arrived, cast around for some way to start a conversation.

'Have you worked for Mr Sutcliffe long?'

The girl gave her an odd look. 'I have been employed by Sutcliffe Trading since I left school,' she said after a short hesitation. Apart from the lisping accent, her English was almost impeccable. 'Naturally, I have only been Mr Brand's assistant for a few months.'

Christy didn't see why that was so natural at all, but somehow Rainbow's answer didn't invite further enquiry. 'What is he like?' she asked next. 'Mr Sutcliffe, I mean.'

'As an employer, Miss Maynard?'

'Yes; yes, of course.' Christy felt flustered by the query. What on earth had Rainbow thought she was asking—what he was like as a lover? The thought was powerfully unsettling, as was the suspicion that Rainbow might well have been able to satisfy her curiosity on that score. Brand obviously relied on her for more than merely secretarial duties. But just how far did their relationship extend?

The Chinese girl's precise English cut off that disturbing train of thought. 'He is not an easy man to work for, but he is fair. And he demands the best.'

She looked at Christy as if wondering how she fitted into that scheme of excellence, and her eyes narrowed. 'Miss Maynard, may I give you a friendly warning? Mr Sutcliffe is a very attractive man, but he has rather a—dangerous reputation with women. It would be better——'

But a sound in the outer office alerted her and she broke off to hurry from the room. Left alone, Christy found her imagination working overtime. Was Brand's reputation such that all female visitors had to be warned off for their own protection? Because that had certainly been a warning. . .

Mixed with her annoyance at Rainbow's assumptions, Christy felt a thrill of apprehension. It was odd that the girl should have used that word 'dangerous'. . . But when Brand re-entered the room she pushed the uncomfortable thought aside. There was nothing dangerous about him now. He appeared to be in high good humour.

'Now that's more like it.' Brand sat down at his desk and leant back, looking up at her with undisguised admiration. 'I did wonder if the suit was a little over the top, but Rainbow assured me——'

'Over the top?' Chisty's voice soared with the release of tension, taxed by the difficulty of fully expressing her anger while keeping her arms firmly crossed. The bra that had been provided with the clothes had been painfully small and unwearable, and the shirt itself was rather tight. She could feel her breasts gently nudging the silk with her slightest movement.

'It's so far over the top that it's halfway up the next hill! I look ridiculous.'

'Don't be silly,' he said placidly. 'In Hong Kong it's hardly possible for a woman to overdress. If you look at my office staff, you'll see that half of them are wearing designer labels—or else extremely good imitations. Don't worry; you look perfect.'

He waved her to a seat on the other side of his mahogany desk. 'And stop hugging yourself like that—there's no need to hide your breasts. They're very attractive.'

'You took my bra!' she ground through clenched

teeth, feeling her face turn crimson. 'The one your—secretary—bought me was far too small.'

'Yes, I'm sorry about that. Chinese women are—rather less well endowed. I'll see you get a replacement.' Brand grinned. 'But in the meantime, I doubt if they'll actually fall off if you let go of them. Or perhaps we could take turns? You may need your hands for taking notes.'

He didn't sound sorry, she thought venomously. He looked as if he was enjoying every moment of her embarrassment. 'So what about the rest of my things? When do I get them back?'

'Now don't be difficult, Christy.' Brand leaned back in his chair, smiling complacently. 'Did you have breakfast by the pool? And did my driver call for you all right?'

'Obviously, since I'm here. And no, I didn't eat by the pool; I called room service. What about my clothes, Brand? You can't just steal them.'

'Oh, you must try the pool breakfast—they do a superb buffet.' And when had he tried it? Christy wondered acidly. Did his 'dangerous reputation' normally extend to seducing his visiting lady experts? 'In future, you'll probably prefer to walk down to the Star Ferry and cross the harbour by boat. Far quicker than the tunnel. But this morning I thought it was advisable for you to arrive in style.'

'Brand——'

'Now what do you want to do? Shall I introduce you round the office first? Or would you like to get straight down to whatever mysterious things you've come here to do?'

Christy gave up. The subject of her clothes would have to wait until later. There was a job to be done, after all—and the sooner she started, the sooner she could return to England. And get back to what was left of her routine.

It should have been a comforting thought. But somehow her old contentment seemed very far away.

Two hours later, Christy's head was spinning with facts and figures. 'So tell me if I've got this right,' she said at last, flicking through the pages of notes she had taken until she came to a fresh sheet. 'Sutcliffe's is basically a merchant company—importing goods from around the East and selling them on.' She drew a neat rectangular box and labelled it 'Trading'. 'But you also own a shipping business——' she drew another box '—which is used by your own trading company——' she drew a line connecting the two boxes '—as well as by outside companies who don't own their own ships.'

He nodded, and she went on adding to the diagram, elaborating it, trying to pull together the information he had given her into some overall pattern. When she had covered the whole page with boxes and interlinked lines, she tore it out and re-drew it all more neatly. Then she pushed it across the desk. 'How does that look?'

Brand gave it a cursory glance. 'Apart from the fact that I've never thought of my company as a collection of little boxes, yes, that seems about right.' There was a note of irritation in his voice that Christy didn't understand.

'What's the matter?' Christy realised that she had

been enjoying the more relaxed atmosphere between them. 'Have I said something to annoy you?'

He shook his head. 'Not really. It's just—God almighty, Christy, how do you stand it? Pick, pick, pick; question after question. And those damn diagrams! Just watching you do it sets my teeth on edge.'

She looked at him for a moment, startled at his vehemence. And then she laughed. Somehow it was comforting to find that there was a chink in Brand Sutcliffe's armour.

'I enjoy it,' she said honestly. 'The finding out— gradually building up a picture. But I've nearly finished with you for the time being. At least. . .'

Christy hesitated for a moment, wondering how he was going to take her prying into what he almost certainly saw as his private business. But it was something that had to be settled. 'Well, actually, there was one other question I wanted to ask. It may not be relevant, but——'

Brand sank back into his seat, clutching his head in an exaggerated gesture of despair. 'Why let that stop you? Ask away. But when the men in white coats come, I shall deduct their charges from your bill.'

'Well, it's just that last night, you mentioned your brother and that he won the company from you—but now you're obviously in charge. So where does he fit in—and do I need to consult him?'

'You're right. It isn't relevant.' Brand's voice was flat now, with no trace of his earlier amusement. 'But there's no real reason why you shouldn't know. My brother's dead. He was killed with his wife in a helicopter accident six months ago. I inherited

Sutcliffe's and I own it outright. I'd have told you last night if you hadn't made it clear that you weren't interested.'

'I'm sorry.' Christy felt a flush of shame as she remembered just how intolerant she had been. 'How terrible—about the accident. You must have been shattered.'

'It came as a shock—but not for the reason you think.' There was a cold bitterness in his eyes which shocked her. 'My brother's death wasn't a personal tragedy. We were never close. In fact I hated his guts— he'd made my life a misery since we were kids. That's why I was willing to risk everything in that damn race. Anything was better than spending the rest of my life with him blocking me at every turn.'

'I don't understand——'

'No, neither did my father. He'd always been blind where Joss and I were concerned. Otherwise he'd never have been so criminally stupid as to leave us in joint control.'

'Of Sutcliffe's?'

'Yes. It was doomed from the start, of course.' Brand leaned back in his chair, staring at a gold pen that he was twisting round and round in his hands. 'Though, to be fair, when my father was alive, we made a reasonable team despite the personal friction. Joss was always one for taking the safe route and I was six years younger and more fiery, so with Dad as a mediator we generally did OK. But without his casting vote we just went round in circles. The company was heading downhill rapidly but neither of us could afford to buy the other one out. Hence the bet.'

'Winner takes all?'

'Oh, no.' The words were bitingly contemptuous. 'My dear brother was never a gambler—and he was too stupid to see that if we carried on the way we were there soon wouldn't be a company to squabble about. No, the odds had to be stacked high on his side to persuade him to play. If he lost, he kept his share of the business but I got a casting vote. Whereas if he won. . .'

'He got everything?'

'That's right. He was a greedy man, my brother.' His voice changed almost imperceptibly, and Christy felt her eyes drawn to his face. 'Greedier even than I thought. . .'

Christy was intrigued. This was the second time Brand had implied that he had lost more than he expected as the result of his bet. Only what else could a man lose, who had already lost everything?

She was tempted to ask. But there was something in his face that didn't invite questions. 'Then that's the lot,' she said briskly. 'That's given me the back-ground—I'll fill in the details later. With your staff,' she added as she saw his look of horror. 'I shouldn't have to put you through another session for the time being.'

'Thank God for that.' His relief was heartfelt. 'In that case, I suggest we have lunch and then you can spend the afternoon shopping. You can start work tomorrow. I'll ask Rainbow to make sure you get all the help and co-operation you need. How does that sound?'

'Fine.' It had been a productive morning, there was

no doubt about that. But as she followed Brand out of the office, Christy's feelings of satisfaction were mixed with unease.

No doubt her reaction was completely unreasonable. But she knew she would have felt much happier if anyone but Rainbow had been charged with smoothing her way. . .

'A successful afternoon, don't you agree?' Brand waved a hand at the packages that surrounded their poolside table. 'And they do a good tea here—all very English. Even you couldn't find smoked salmon and cucumber sandwiches excessively exotic.'

Christy nodded, ignoring his teasing. She had been surprised to realise just how much she had enjoyed herself. Although she had been secretly appalled when, over lunch, Brand had declared his intention of accompanying her on her shopping expedition, she had to admit that it had turned out more pleasure than ordeal.

With his local knowledge, Brand had known exactly where to take her and in less than two hours she had more than replaced the lost contents of her luggage— as well as being measured for another suit, which the tailor assured her would be ready for an initial fitting the next day.

Christy hadn't yet had the courage to work out how much her extravagance had cost, but she knew that Mike would agree she had done the right thing. Her London clothes would have made her look drab as a sparrow among the Hong Kong women, who flocked the streets like brightly coloured birds.

Mentally flicking through the new additions to her wardrobe, Christy realised that the clothes Rainbow had supplied had mysteriously influenced her own selection. It was as if the peacock-blue suit's extravagance had somehow seeped into her bones.

She had intended to go for quiet elegance—a look to which Brand couldn't possibly object, but which would show him that she intended to make her own choice. A sort of designer version of the infamous grey suit, in fact. But the blue silk had turned up its nose and now the hangers jostled with sun-bright colours.

Except, that was, for the dress.

The dress was black; black silk, skin-tight to the knees and totally impractical, hemmed with a froth of lace that rustled against her calves. Christy shivered as she remembered the sensuous touch of the softly luxurious fabric. The fit had been perfect; it could have been made for her. It hadn't mattered that it was totally unlike anything she had ever worn—she had known as soon as she saw it that it would look stunning.

Sipping the tea in its elegant china cup, she looked sideways at Brand, as if he might have been reading her thoughts, but he was engrossed in a newspaper the waiter had brought with the tea. His eyes scanned columns of figures that Christy assumed must be stockmarket results, the concentration creasing his forehead like a frown.

Brand didn't know about the dress. When Christy had seen it hanging in a shop window, she had said nothing, wanting to keep it secret for some reason that she didn't even try to understand.

Not until he had left her for a few minutes to do

some shopping of his own had she rushed back to try it
on greedily. Wearing it had been an almost sensual
experience, buying it a foregone conclusion. Even the
frighteningly high price-tag had done nothing to lessen
its appeal.

Halfway through her second sandwich, Christy
started to feel that she was being watched. It was a
strange, unsettling sensation and she looked round
surreptitiously to see if she could spot the cause of it.
But the other guests seemed innocently self-absorbed;
and the windows looking out on the pool were blank
and empty.

And then she saw it. A flicker of movement in the
flower-bed by the wall—a flash of striped fur. And
then just the tip of a tail twitching impatiently on the
brown earth. It was the cat she had seen from her
window that morning. The pool was obviously a regular
hunting ground.

Brand hadn't seen it. Feeling rather foolish, Christy
picked a piece of salmon out of her sandwich and
dropped it, mock accidentally, so that it fell close to
the lurker's watching place. A ginger paw flashed out—
so quickly that she might have missed it. And the
morsel was gone.

Her own hunger almost forgotten in the fascination
of the game, Christy continued trying to tempt her
unseen companion out of hiding. The pieces of salmon
fell further and further from the bushes and nearer and
nearer to her table, and yet her opponent still kept up
the pretence of concealment. Until a particularly large
slice dropped right under her chair. . .

There was no reaction at first, except that the tail tip

seemed to twitch a little more frenetically. Christy found herself holding her breath. And then slowly the bushes parted and a pair of startlingly yellow eyes peered up at her, as if trying to gauge the trustworthiness of this unexpectedly co-operative source of sustenance. She must have passed the test. The cat darted out and crouched beneath the table, growling quietly.

'Oh, you poor thing!' The little animal was so thin that its fur seemed just laid across a rack of bones, and as she bent down to stroke it, Christy realised that one side of its face was swollen and weeping, the fur matted with dried blood. And there was something else wrong. The piece of fish it had so coveted lay scarcely touched between its dirty paws.

'What's the matter, little one? Is it too big?' Hurriedly, Christy tore what remained of the filling of her sandwich into tiny pieces, and this new offering was warmly received. A small pink tongue flickered in and out, and what sounded like a small motorbike engine stirred into life by Christy's foot.

'You poor darling. Is something wrong with your mouth?' Christy bent forwards again to try and examine it more closely, but the cat backed away with a nervous hiss.

'Don't touch it, you little idiot. It's probably got every disease in the book.'

Christy started back in shock. She had almost forgotten Brand's presence in her preoccupation with the cat. The little animal tensed, and its purring stopped. But after a few seconds, hunger overcame fear, and it didn't resort to flight.

'Shhh! Don't frighten it—it's injured, I think. Look, on its jaw.'

But to her surprise, Brand scarcely gave it a glance. 'I was just thinking I could take you racing tonight, at Happy Valley,' he said, spreading the paper on the table so that she could see that the columns of figures she had taken for stock-market results were actually tables of odds. 'There's a twilight meeting, and I've promised to see some people there. I'll be going on afterwards, but I'll put you in a taxi back. How about it?'

'What?' Christy hardly listened to what he was saying. 'Oh, don't bother me about that now, Brand. I told you; I'm not into sightseeing. What am I going to do about this cat?'

Brand frowned. 'Hong Kong isn't the place to get sentimental about stray animals, Christy. Or domesticated ones, for that matter. You'll only upset yourself.'

'I'm not getting sentimental!' The charge stung her. 'But you can see it's hurt. And it's so thin—but no wonder, when it can hardly eat. It's starving to death, Brand.'

'And so are thousands of other cats—you can't help them all. It's just natural selection—the weakest die off and the strongest breed. You don't help anything by interfering, except perhaps yourself. It's kindest to let nature take its course.'

'I don't see why the fact that there are thousands of others should make any difference,' she retorted stubbornly. He sounded so—implacable, like a force of nature himself. And his callousness appalled her. 'Maybe I can't help them all—but I can help this one.'

The words were out before she knew she was going to say them. 'I'm going to take him to the vet.'

'And what will that accomplish? Even supposing you could find a vet willing to treat it, that is?'

'What do you mean, what will it accomplish? He's got some sort of abscess, I think. If the vet can fix it up, he'll be able to eat again. It might save his life.'

'And then he'll die of something else. It won't work, Christy. If the vet gave him antibiotics against this, it would just weaken him against a hundred other infections. If he hasn't got the constitution to survive on his own; you're not doing him any favours by dragging it out. Remember, he hasn't got an indulgent mistress to pamper him till he's back on his feet.'

'So you think I should just ignore him? Watch him suffer?'

Brand bent down to look more closely at the injury. Then he pulled out a chair and sat down. 'If you genuinely want to save him suffering,' he said more gently, 'then the best thing to do would be to have the vet put him down. I think that jaw might be broken. It looks to me as if he's been kicked.'

She pounced on the admission. 'Then you do know of a vet? Couldn't we just see if there's anything he could do?'

'It's a she.'

Oh, yes—it would be, Christy thought. 'In that case, I'm sure she'd be delighted to do you a favour,' she said, with a touch of sarcasm that she instantly regretted. 'Oh, please, Brand,' she pleaded, changing tack. 'I can't just walk off and leave him now.'

At first, she was sure he was going to refuse. 'On one condition,' he said at last.

'Which is?' There was a strange expression on his face which made her suspicious.

'That you come racing with me this evening.' He grinned. 'Lesson one in the art of living dangerously.'

CHAPTER FOUR

'I DON'T understand why you're doing this, Brand.'

Christy followed him out through the car park, where every car seemed to be either a Rolls or a Mercedes, and through a turnstile into the course's luxurious stands. The little gold badge he had given her to wear hung by its red cord from her buttonhole, tapping against her breast as she hurried at his heels.

'I've already told you I'd much rather have an early night. What possible difference can it make to you whether or not I go horse-racing?'

She felt hot and flustered despite the air-conditioning, and was already regretting the bargain she had struck. After all, she could have found a vet herself—although how she would have managed to catch and transport an enraged cat without Brand's help, she was rather less sure.

In her head, she could still hear the yowling that Mauw—christened at her insistence and to Brand's disgust with the Cantonese word for 'cat'—had set up in vigorous protest against the indignities of veterinary medicine.

Brand shrugged. 'I might as well ask what difference it makes to you whether one stray cat out of thousands lives or dies.'

'That's hardly the same. Mauw was hurt; I felt sorry for him, that's all.'

'Or else you wanted to play God. Well, either of those reasons would do as well for me. Let's say I just felt sorry for you.'

'How dare you? I don't want your pity!'

'From the racket he was making, your protégé didn't want yours. Neither of you have any choice.' Brand quickened his pace and she had to hurry to keep up with him. 'Someone once kicked you, Christy, and it left an abscess on your courage, not your jaw. Perhaps I just like the idea of being the one to save your life.'

'You're being ridiculous.' Christy felt herself going pink. 'No one ever died of an aversion to tourism. Lots of people live perfectly happy lives without ever leaving the place they were born.'

'But you're not living a perfectly happy life, are you?' He swung round suddenly, so that she almost cannoned into him. The anger in his voice took her aback. 'In fact, what you're doing would hardly qualify as living at all. These people you talk about have families, friends. What do you have? A partner who's married and a dead cat.'

'Don't be silly. I've got friends,' she protested.

'Have you? Then how come the other evening you told me you didn't have anyone to talk to?'

Christy flushed as she remembered just how thoroughly she had given herself away. 'I was jet-lagged,' she muttered. 'And besides, they're just not that sort of friends.'

'Then they're not friends at all.' Brand turned abruptly off the main corridor and up some stairs. 'What about your family?'

'What about them? I have got one, if that's what you're asking.' Christy forced a smile. The last thing she wanted was to confirm his suspicions, or he'd never leave her alone. 'In fact I saw my father only a few days ago.'

'Did you, indeed.' Brand's tone was unexpectedly thoughtful, and Christy felt her heart sink. He really was dangerously perceptive, and the last thing she wanted was to get into a discussion about her father. She just wanted to put him out of her mind.

'It's really none of your business how I live my life, Brand,' she hurried on before he could quiz her any further. 'And I wish you'd leave me alone. Where on earth are you taking me anyway?'

They had entered a large hall, one side of which was lined with service windows, like a ticket-office or a bank. Behind the glass, one for each window, she could see a row of computer terminals. But there was no one in sight and Christy suddenly realised that they hadn't seen another person since passing through the turnstile. The effect was disconcerting, like a sort of technological Mary Celeste.

Her reaction must have shown on her face. Brand grinned. 'It won't be deserted for long. We're a bit early, but I want to miss the traffic. What are you afraid of, Christy? Mysterious Chinamen?'

'Perhaps.' She tried to laugh, but it didn't sound convincing. *Danger.* Even at their first meeting she had seen him as dangerous. 'Perhaps I'm afraid of you.' Oh, God, why had she said that?

'Are you?' He turned to look at her with an intensity in his eyes that she recognised. She had seen it before—reflected in the door at the hotel restaurant. But now she was seeing it direct.

A burning. . . 'Are you afraid of me, Christy?'

He took a step towards her and reached out a hand. She wanted to back away; to run; to escape. But she could do nothing. She stood transfixed as he ran his fingers deep into the mass of her hair, twisting it to the edge of pain, pulling her towards him.

'I hope you are,' he said softly. He was close; so close. His eyes were all she could see. And his mouth. . . 'You should be afraid. I'm going to drag you out of your safe little burrow, Christy.' His mouth was poised over hers and his words buzzed on her lips. 'I'm going to teach you to live.'

'No!' But the plea was in her mind; not on her lips. Her lips were smothered into silence by the dominating softness of his mouth as it caressed hers; subduing it with a pleasure that had nothing to do with wanting or not wanting, nothing to do with choice. A pleasure that turned her legs to water, a careless flame that set her senses ablaze.

This was what she had seen in his eyes. . . The thought spun through her mind, a brief flash of clarity in the whirlwind. This was what she had feared. Somehow she had known he had this power. In her dreams, she had known it. Only this was no dream. . .

'No!' She had to resist the sweetness that spread through her mind like a numbing drug, sapping her will. 'Brand. . .' But the only sound that came was a moan of pleasure, and he pulled her closer, his free hand moulding her hips against the taut muscle of his thighs.

The liquid warmth of desire within her devoured thought, devoured shame. She could hear his breathing, harsh as a runner's in his chest as she swayed against him, and her hands clung to the damp cotton of his shirt. As if he were the rock which might save her instead of the tide which swept her away.

But then a door swung open and there was a sudden clatter of footsteps in the emptiness of the hall behind them.

'Good evening, Mr Sutcliffe—Miss Maynard.' The familiar lisping voice was dipped in acid, and Christy jerked herself free from Brand's embrace as if she had been stung. But Rainbow was already walking away from them towards a door on the far side of the room, her mincing steps exuding disapproval.

Christy felt her cheeks flame with horrified embarrassment. There could be no doubt what the girl had seen. 'Now look what you've done!' She tried to calm her ragged breathing without much success, keenly aware of the wanton spectacle she must be presenting. With one nervous hand she patted her hair back into shape, as if that small measure of control might help to banish the greater chaos that had so nearly overwhelmed her.

'Brand, I don't—we aren't——You must explain to Rainbow——'

'Explain what? Look at yourself.' His hand slid down to touch her breast, brushing deliberately against the hardened peak of her nipple. 'You want me, Christy. The way I want you. That's all the explanation I need.'

She opened her mouth in denial; then closed it again. The blood that still clamoured in her cheeks made an easy answer impossible. What did she want? And what was it about this man that let him walk through her defences like so much tissue paper?

His reckless forcefulness represented everything she most feared; everything she knew instinctively was most dangerous to her hard-won security. If she let go, almost anything might happen. And yet she knew that to him, she was nothing but a temporary amusement. A challenge.

And yet. . . There was something in his piratical attitude that made the danger seem almost seductive. Like the man. . .

Brand smiled slowly at her silent confusion, as if he could read her thoughts. 'That's lesson one.' His voice still stirred a thrill of excitement inside her. 'There'll be a test on it later. But now we'd better join Rainbow in the box. The rest of the party will be arriving soon and I want to show you the ropes before the first race.'

He turned as if to set off towards the door through which Rainbow had disappeared, but Christy hung back in a panic.

'Brand, I can't go in there now. Please, couldn't you take me home? What will she think?'

'She'll think a great deal more if we disappear off together.' Brand seemed to be rather amused than embarrassed by his secretary's interruption. 'Unless that's what you have in mind, of course. . .' He looked down at her mockingly and Christy felt herself blush again with shame. 'In which case I'll be delighted to oblige.'

'Oh!' For a moment, she thought of turning round and making her own way back to the hotel. But at the back of her mind was the fear that he wouldn't let her go; that he might try to stop her. That he might touch her again. . . And if that happened——

It mustn't happen. Giving her hair another pat to compose herself, she headed with grim determination towards the door.

To Christy's surprise, the room Brand ushered her into looked more like a small restaurant than the stadium-type stand she had been expecting. A sumptuous-looking buffet was spread along the length of one wall and a number of elegantly set round tables took up the greater part of the room. Their silver cutlery and sparkling glasswear danced with light from the central chandelier.

Only the warm breeze from the door to the open balcony and the panoramic view of the racecourse spread out below recalled the purpose of their visit, and Christy felt a little happier. She had imagined something much more sordid, like back-street bookmakers in England, not this brightly lit and almost opulent scene.

Even Rainbow's presence seemed somehow less of a threat. After all, it was not the Chinese girl whom Brand settled in the prime seat facing the window—and beside his own. It was Rainbow who was excluded while her boss explained in detail to Christy the various odds and different ways of betting.

'You can bet on one horse; to come first or in the first three—that's a place. Or you could try a Forecast, which means trying to pick the first two horses in any one race. . .' Brand leaned across to point out the details in the 'Betting Guide' he had obtained for her, his hand brushing lightly against the skin of her arm.

His closeness revived precisely the memories she was trying most desperately to suppress—a reaction which she suspected Brand of deliberately provoking. But despite her emotional confusion, Christy found she was listening all the more avidly to his explanations because of her awareness of Rainbow's annoyance.

She felt a sting of shame at the pleasure her petty victory gave her—particularly since she had no intention of wasting money on betting in any case—but it was something she couldn't suppress. It occurred to her that Brand might be deliberately trying to make the Chinese girl jealous. Or was she wrong, and the two were not lovers at all?

She was taken aback at the relief that accompanied that thought. What was it to her whom Brand Sutcliffe consorted with in his leisure hours? She could hardly suppose him to be celibate. There was nothing in his vital and overwhelmingly masculine body to suggest asceticism—far from it. And whether Rainbow was one of them or not, he would have no shortage of willing partners. . .

Hastily, Christy fixed her mind on Brand's explanation of something called a 'treble', trying to shut out the qualms that vision brought.

At last he sat back, presumably confident that he had taught her all she needed to know, although in fact most of her attention had been on Rainbow's reaction and the bustle in the room.

All through her lesson in betting theory, Christy had been aware that the place was filling up. By now, all the tables except their own were full, and uniformed stewards were hovering to serve the drinks.

'Don't worry, little rabbit,' Brand whispered wickedly in her ear as they stood up to approach the buffet. 'There won't be anything to frighten you here.' He was right: the food on the long table was very English in style, despite the fact that about half the diners were Chinese.

'What a strange way to run a restaurant, though,' Christy said innocently as she finished her sweet. 'No menu to choose from or anything. But I suppose people don't really come here for the food.'

Rainbow burst out giggling behind one elegantly manicured hand. 'This is not a restaurant, Miss Maynard. This is Mr Sutcliffe's private box. These people are all clients or business colleagues or Mr Sutcliffe.'

'Oh, I see.' Christy felt her face redden again as her confidence dropped away. 'I'm sorry, I didn't realise——'

'Why should you?' Brand smiled and Christy felt her rival stiffen at the implied rebuke.

Her rival? Where on earth had that come from? She was letting herself be brainwashed by Brand's own forceful perceptions of their relationship. He was just her client, and the Chinese girl was welcome to him—if she could get him. There was no way Christy was going to set up in competition.

Except that, just then, Rainbow leaned across the table, her high, flirtatious voice whispering to Brand in rapid Cantonese. Christy felt immediately certain that she was the subject under discussion and a sideways glance from Rainbow's almond-shaped eyes was enough to provide conviction. She felt a surge of irritation.

Perhaps she had been infected by the atmosphere of reckless excitement in the stadium as the stands filled up and the horses were parading round the collecting ring in preparation for the first race, but it suddenly seemed irrelevant that she didn't want Brand for herself. Christy was seized by a rebellious determination that, for tonight at least, the Chinese girl shouldn't have it all her own way with her cryptic warnings and catty remarks.

If Rainbow wanted a fight, she could have one—and on her own terms.

'Oh, do call me Christy, Rainbow.' Her decision to be as offensive as possible gave Christy an exhilarating sense of freedom. 'I'm sure Mr Sutcliffe wouldn't mind, would you, Brand?' That was nicely done, underlining the contrast between Rainbow's 'working' relationship and her own supposed intimacy. Christy felt she was getting into her stride.

She carried on talking with as much of her back

turned to Rainbow as she could manage—even if it did look as if she was trying to twine herself around Brand Sutcliffe's arm. 'This is hardly a formal occasion, after all,' she cooed. 'I'm sure you must allow your staff a little latitude outside work.'

The effect on Rainbow was all she could have hoped. Christy was beginning to see through the apparent impassivity of the Chinese girl's expression. The signs were less obvious than they would have been on a Western face, but they were unmistakable. The atmosphere around the little table was beginning to sizzle.

'Oh, certainly—let's not stand on ceremony.' Brand's half-smile convinced Christy that he guessed what she was up to. Well, let him guess—even if it did lead him to believe that she was a serious contender for his favours. She would soon disillusion him if he tried anything.

A quaver of doubt that rose as she remembered the last time he had 'tried something' was quickly suppressed. That time, she had been taken by surprise. It couldn't happen again. And it would do Brand Sutcliffe good to realise that there was at least one woman in the world who wasn't prepared to throw herself at his feet—despite the natural physical reaction he was no doubt so used to arousing.

'Christy, then.' Rainbow's voice was sweet as honey, with its slight but attractive stumbling on the 'r' of the name, but Christy could feel the waves of hostility that accompanied the words and knew that her patronising tone had struck home.

'That's better. We're bound to be seeing such a lot

of each other, after all—we ought to be friends. And perhaps I can help you with your English—it's really quite good, but there are one or two things I've noticed that you could work on. . .'

'I don't think I've ever seen my secretary so angry,' Brand said in amusement a little later. Rainbow had finally tired of having her pronunciation corrected every time she opened her mouth and had wandered off to join one of the other groups as soon as the racing started.

'You don't object, then?' Christy looked at him sideways to assess his reaction. 'I'd hate to—spoil anything for you. I rather think she was looking to you for support.'

'Oh, Rainbow can look after herself, believe me.' The urbane comment gave Christy no clues as to his real attitude. Was he just so confident of his powers that he enjoyed pitting 'his' women against each other? Or was he really indifferent? 'I just hope you know what you're doing,' he went on. 'You've got to work with her, after all. But I must admit that I'm flattered.'

'Well, you needn't be.' Christy's response was tart. 'I can assure you that I'm not doing it for the pleasure of your unadulterated company. But as for working with her, I thought it might be a little easier in the long run if I demonstrated that she couldn't walk all over me whenever she felt like it. I'd heard of the army phrase "dumb insolence", but I don't think I'd ever experienced it before.'

'So the rabbit has teeth?' He looked at her musingly. 'Well, now you've routed my secretary, I'm afraid it's up to you to entertain me, like it or not. So I suggest we go out on to the balcony for the next race. And isn't it about time you took the plunge and placed your first bet?'

All around them there was an atmosphere of mingled jubilation and disappointment as the results of the race just run were subjected to passionate analysis.

Christy looked around her in distaste. It was all so reminiscent of one of her father's 'business gatherings', when he and whoever his colleagues might be for a particular venture would descend on the house to drink champagne and convince themselves that one particular success was worth all the failures that had inevitably preceded it. 'I've picked a horse—number eight—and I shall just support it in my head,' she said firmly. That the horse was called Buccaneer was just another of those coincidences that she didn't want to investigate too closely. After all, you had to pick them out for some kind of reason. And the fact that the horse in question had looked big, black and very full of itself when walking round the collecting ring had somehow confirmed her in her choice. 'I don't need to throw money away to enjoy myself,' she added crushingly—although, in fact, she wasn't enjoying herself much at all. Watching a bunch of horses running round a track was hardly her idea of gripping entertainment—particularly since they were so far away that she could hardly make out the jockeys' colours. And watching it on the great closed-circuit screen that dominated the centre of the concourse seemed even more futile. She might as well have stayed in the hotel and watched the whole thing on television—an option that had far greater appeal.

'Now that is where you are wrong, little rabbit.' Brand took her by the elbow and started to steer her back out towards the mian hall. 'You're bored stiff— and that's because racing without betting is like drinking champagne after a dental anaesthetic. The Sport of Kings is not something you watch—it's something you experience. And you can't do that if you've got nothing riding on the outcome.'

'Brand, will you leave me alone? It's all right for you, but I can't afford——' She became aware that the queues of people that had formed at the previously deserted 'ticket offices' were all turning to look at her curiously, and lowered her voice to a hiss. 'This is ridiculous, Brand. Let go of my arm.'

'Certainly—so long as you promise to behave yourself. These people won't be very pleased if you delay their placing of their bets.'

They were nearly at the glass window now, and reluctantly Christy gave her assent. 'But I'm not going to risk my company's money on——'

'Quite right; you're going to risk mine. Ah——' The queue shuffled forward and they found themselves standing by the window, the clerk's fingers poised over the computer keys.

'The lady would like a hundred dollars on number eight for the next race. Win and place.' Brand pulled a wallet from an inside pocket, drew off a couple of notes and slid them over the counter, receiving in exchange a small punched card which he handed to Christy as they moved away.

'Brand, I don't want this! It may be chicken-feed to you, but I think it's ridiculous to waste a hundred dollars on——'

'Two hundred dollars.' He shook his head mockingly. 'Weren't you listening to anything I said earlier on? The bet was "win and place"—that means you have to pay double the stake. Whereas if you'd just——'

'Oh, for goodness' sake! How do I get it through to you that I'm just not interested?' She tried to hand back the card, but he wouldn't take it.

'No, that's yours. Like it or not, if that horse comes in, you're going to be a little bit richer, Christy. At least until you lose it all on the next race. Don't make such a fuss; it's hardly a fortune. That meal we ate last night cost considerably more. Just loosen up, will you? It's almost time for the starter's orders.'

As they made their way back to the box and out on to the balcony, Christy reflected in frustration that one sensation she was becoming increasingly familiar with was knowing when she was beaten. No matter how petty the issue, Brand Sutcliffe somehow managed to ride roughshod over anything—and anyone—who stood up against him. He really was a most insufferable man.

'And it's Tai Tai; Tai Tai and Jade Dragon. Tai Tai, Jade Dragon and Buccaneer. And Buccaneer is coming up on Jade Dragon; it's Tai Tai, Jade Dragon and Buccaneer; Tai Tai, Buccaneer and Jade Dragon; Tai Tai and Buccaneer are neck and neck—Buccaneer——'

'Go on, Buccaneer!' Christy heard a voice shouting for her horse, and one part of her brain registered with astonishment that it was her own. The rest of her was clinging to the rail at the front of the balcony, jumping up and down with the sheer excitement of the closely run finish.

'And it's Buccaneer first; Buccaneer first and Tai Tai second and Jade Dragon third. Buccaneer, Tai Tai and Jade Dragon.'

Despite herself, she let out a whoop of glee. 'I've won! I've won! Oh, Brand—how much will it come to? What do I do? Can I go and collect my winnings now?'

'If you'd listened to your teacher, you'd be able to work it out,' he said with mock severity. 'But don't worry—it will come up on the board in a minute. Don't forget you collect twice; once for a win and once for a place. But it's definitely worth a celebration.'

He signalled to a steward who hurried forward with a bottle of champagne and a tray of glasses. 'Look—there it is.' Breaking off from the act of pouring for a moment, Brand gestured with the bottle to the results board, where the numbers were rolling over to indicate the final totals.

'See it? Where it says "win". That's for a ten-dollar stake, so you'll get ten times that. And there's the place as well. . . That's——'

But for once Christy's mind was working at lightning speed. 'That's almost a thousand dollars! Oh, Brand—I'm sorry I was so stuffy. You were right, it is a lot of fun this way.'

Dimly, in her euphoria, she was aware that she would probably regret this admission in the future, but the excitement was frothing up inside her like the champagne bubbles in her glass. 'Can I really keep it? I'd like to put some on the next race. What was that Forecast thing you were talking about? Next time, I think I might try one of those.'

By the end of the evening, Christy was surprised to find that her mood was hardly dampened, despite the fact that her first win had been the only successful result of the night. She had become almost expert in marking out cards for the different varieties of bet and, although her own stakes were far more modest than Brand's original bet on her behalf and she was still well within her winnings, that didn't seem to affect the excitement she felt.

One or two of her horses had come close, only to flag in the last few furlongs. But now, in the last race, she was determined to make a good choice.

'Which do you think, Brand? Golden Emperor or Lucky Legs? I can't decide, and they're both about the same odds.'

Brand shrugged. 'Back both then, if you like. But given the success you had with Buccaneer, perhaps you ought to go for number three.'

'Number three?' She traced it down on her programme. 'Cheung Po Tsai? Why that one?'

'Because Cheung Po Tsai was one of Hong Kong's most famous pirates. He used to lord it over one of the islands; a place called Cheung Chow. I'll have to take you there; it's a fascinating place.'

'I'd like that.' The words were out before she could stop them, but once she had said them she realised it was the truth. 'How would we get there? By boat?'

'Unless rabbits are better swimmers than I thought, yes. In fact, normally I'd take you over in my own boat, *Moondancer*, but the radio's packed up at the moment and I'm waiting for spares. But we could take the ferry across. What about Saturday? It's hardly worth it unless we take the whole day.'

Saturday. Christy had been planning on spending Saturday getting all her paperwork in order, but the thought of a day out of the city was certainly tempting. 'All right,' she said impulsively. 'Thank you. And now I'd better go and place my bet on this pirate.'

She was just on her way back with her card held tightly in her hand, pushing through the now crowded balcony to find Brand, when she was surprised to see him pushing out the opposite way.

'What's up?' she said in puzzlement. 'You'll miss the start if you're not careful.'

'Sorry, Christy,' he grimaced. 'I'm going to have to leave, but I'll get the steward to organise you a taxi. Rainbow's just pointed out that we'll be late if I don't go now.'

He gestured behind her, and Christy swung round to see the Chinese girl, with a catlike smile of satisfaction on her face, waiting by the door with a fur wrap draped elegantly over her narrow shoulders.

It was like stepping back into the real world. Christy realised that for the last few hours she had been behaving like someone in a dream. She had let him hypnotise her. . . A surge of anger came to her aid. No wonder Rainbow had given up so easily. She had known she would have the last laugh.

'So after forcing me to put up with your company all evening you're now just going to walk off and leave me stranded, are you?' she flared. 'Very gentlemanly, Mr Sutcliffe.'

Brand's lips tightened with anger. 'Is that what you were doing? Putting up with me?' And before she could slap his hand away, he had reached out and touched her breast, watching insolently as the nipple hardened beneath the silk. The reminder was obvious.

'I look forward to seeing you enjoy yourself, in that case. It should be quite an experience.'

'You caught me off guard, that's all.' Somewhere in the background, a roar went up, but whether the pirate had won or lost, Christy no longer cared. 'I'm obviously still jet-lagged—and I didn't expect to be attacked in a public place by a man who is supposed to be my client. I think we'd better just forget about this sightseeing trip on Saturday, Brand. I don't think it would be a good idea.'

Brand's eyes hardened. 'Well I do. And you agreed to it. I'll pick you up from the hotel on Saturday morning.'

'And if I refuse?' But the words died on her lips. Both he and the vet had plainly thought treating a stray cat a waste of time and money. There was no need to ask what would happen if she abandoned her stake in its welfare. 'Oh, what's the point?' she said at last. 'I'll spend the day with you, if you insist. Although why you want to, I haven't the faintest idea. But if you dare touch me again, I'll——'

'You'll what? Put up with me? I can hardly wait. But don't worry, little rabbit. I won't kiss you again. Or at least——'

He grinned, almost wolfishly, she thought wildly. And I'm Little Red Riding Hood. . .

'At least, not till you ask me nicely. And you will.'

CHAPTER FIVE

OVER the next two days, Christy saw very little of her infuriating client. He seemed to be out of the office most of the time, sweeping in only occasionally to collect papers or make arrangements for meetings. It was probably just as well; she might have found it difficult to be civil. Particularly since Rainbow had come in late on Thursday morning, wearing a smile like a cat with shares in a dairy—and displaying with indecent pride a heavy gold charm-bracelet that Brand had given her as a 'thank-you'.

Apart from this, however, Christy could find no real fault with the Chinese girl's behaviour. As if satisfied by such concrete evidence of her victory, she no longer bothered to make jibes at Christy's expense, and took part efficiently in the data-gathering exercise that Christy had set under way in preparation for the new computer's arrival.

So it was probably not deliberate that the bracelet hung down just sufficiently to tap continuously on the desk-top while Rainbow was typing. Unfortunately, it grated just as much on Christy's tense nerves as if it had been deliberate provocation, and by Friday afternoon she was almost ready to strangle the girl with her own typewriter ribbon.

To calm herself down, she decided to walk back to the hotel via the vet's surgery, and find out for herself how the patient was doing. The vet told her that Mauw was well on the mend; his jaw had turned out not to be broken and antibiotics had got the abscess well under control. In a week or so, he should be ready for re-release.

She thanked the woman and asked her to make sure that Christy herself was called when it was time for Mauw to go free. And on the way home she mulled over a plan of action to ensure the little cat didn't have to return to his half-wild existence.

The hotel had a kennels in the basement where visitors' pets could be accommodated during their stay. Instead of releasing him, she would take him back there. And then, after quarantine, he could join her in England and take Sam's place in her flat—and her heart.

The thought gave Christy a glow of satisfaction. Mauw would never be hungry again, never have to scavenge for his food through dustbins and hunt rats in rubbish-piles. He could grow plump and placid like Sam, surrounded by love and luxury. And at least some good would have come out of this terrible trip.

When Saturday morning dawned, Christy assumed that Brand would have forgotten his promise—or threat—to take her out for the day. Their relations since the racing had been distant in the extreme, and in view of his apparent reconciliation with Rainbow she could scarcely believe that the plan would still be of interest.

So it came as quite a shock to be paged in the

middle of a late and rather leisurely breakfast and dragged down to reception where Brand was pacing impatiently up and down the marble floor.

'I thought I told you we'd have to make an early start,' he demanded as she appeared. 'If we're going to make Cheung Chow for lunch we ought to catch the eleven o'clock ferry at the latest.'

'Brand, is there really any point? I really don't want to, and I was planning to go into work. There's a lot still to do——'

'All the more reason to take a day off. You've had a hard week, on top of a long flight. You need to rest or you'll start making mistakes. You seemed very jumpy in the office on Friday.'

So he had noticed her existence, then. 'I could have a rest here.'

'But you wouldn't, would you? And besides, I need a rest too, and showing you round is one way to make sure I get one. For goodness' sake, don't make such an issue of it. You'll enjoy it, Christy— just as you enjoyed the horse-racing.'

'And what about Rainbow?'

'What about her? She doesn't work at weekends— it costs me enough to get her to work overtime during the week.' He sounded genuinely puzzled and for a moment Christy wondered if she could possibly have misunderstood. But then she remembered the bracelet; that was proof enough. She opened her mouth to protest again, but his voice overruled her.

'I don't intend to take no for an answer, Christy.

Go and get your swimsuit and be down in five minutes. What you're wearing will do fine.'

As the wraparound skirt and cotton top she was wearing was just about her only casual outfit, it would have to, thought Christy resentfully as she walked back to the lifts. Their shopping trip had concentrated mainly on working clothes, and one of the things she had planned for the afternoon was a trip to Marks and Spencer to buy some more everyday garments. But it was obvious that this would now have to go by the board.

Like everything else that clashed with Brand Sutcliffe's plans.

As the Rolls drew away into the teeming traffic, Christy found herself gripped firmly by the elbow and guided by Brand into what looked at first sight like an aimlessly milling crowd.

But as they pushed their way into it, the 'crowd' turned out to be a set of distinct queues for the various destinations served by the Outlying Islands ferry terminal. Only 'queues' didn't seem quite the right word to describe this jostling mass of people, each individually determined to push their way six inches further forward than was physically possible. . .

Christy yelped as a white-haired old woman forced her way between them, nearly knocking them over with the huge basket of vegetables she had strapped to her back.

'For goodness' sake!' The exclamation burst out louder than she had expected, and several people looked round. Christy realised that she was over-reacting—no wonder, when the real object of her irritation was so impervious to any kind of reason. . .

'Why on earth can't people just wait their turn?' she said with more control.

'If you lived in a city with one of the highest population densities on earth, would you be so keen on waiting your turn?'

The closing of ranks as the old woman forced past had left them jammed so closely together that Christy could feel his breath gently stirring the hair on top of her head. 'I'd have thought that made it all the more important. This is chaos!'

Brand shook his head. 'That's because you're used to an environment where there's always enough of everything. The first thing any Hong Kong Chinese learns is that he who pushes hardest gets the best of whatever's going. It's a very competitive society, and a queue is an ideal battleground.'

'You sound as if you approve of it.'

He shrugged. 'I suppose I do. If there's only a limited supply of something then anyone who hangs back waiting for it to be handed to him on a plate is a fool. Why shouldn't it go to the one who strains every nerve and sinew and uses every ounce of influence to get it? I've never been afraid to fight for what I wanted.'

'And if you lose?'

His hand went to the scar on his cheek. 'I did, remember?' he said bitterly. And then they were at the barrier and Brand was asking for two tickets to

Cheung Chow. And Christy was wondering just what had burned such pain into his eyes.

'Look at that. The biggest cigarette packet in the world.'

Christy followed the line of Brand's tanned arm, trying to ignore his closeness as he leant across to point towards one of the buildings on the slowly receding shoreline. The whole thing had been painted to resemble a famous brand of cigarettes. The illusion had the curious effect of seeming to alter the scale of its surroundings, making the other buildings look like toys.

Christy laughed with genuine pleasure. 'That's amazing. How on earth did they manage that? Surely it must be against every building regulation in the book?'

'In Hong Kong, everything is possible.' His tone was joking, but there was an underlying note of seriousness. 'There are probably fewer rules and regulations here than any other major city in the world—that's what makes it such an exciting place to do business. You can do almost anything here, if you want it enough.' His voice changed a little as he added, 'And if you can afford it.'

The bitterness was back, and once again Christy found herself wondering what it was he had lost that had hurt him so badly. Somehow, despite his tycoon image, she couldn't imagine Brand Sutcliffe caring deeply enough about money to feel such rancour at a mere financial loss. There was something so vital about him—he would never be down for long. And

besides, his brother's death had surely recouped his
fortunes. . .

'Brand?'

'Mmm?'

'What's that island over there?' It wasn't what she
had meant to say, and Christy felt half ashamed at
her own cowardice. But at the last moment, the
danger signs had flashed back up. This man is
dangerous. . .

'That one to starboard? That's Stonecutters. And
the one just ahead is Siu Tsing Chau—Little Green
Island. And Green Island behind it.'

'They look beautiful, rising out of the water like
that. Like sea-monsters.'

Brand looked at her in surprise. 'The Chinese
would agree with you; to them, all hills are dragons.
That's what Kowloon means—Nine Dragons. But it's
a very un-Christy-like thought.' He added teasingly.
'Perhaps there's hope for you yet.'

'Pig.' But she felt the tension between them evaporate. Christy wasn't sure herself what had inspired
her flight of fancy, but it was as if she was seeing the
landscape around her with new eyes. 'What does
Hong Kong mean, then?'

'Fragrant Harbour.' He grinned at her moué of
disgust. 'The Fragrant bit may not seem all that
appropriate these days, but as a harbour it's unsur-
passed—even in a typhoon. Before they invented
reinforced concrete and typhoon shelters, they used
to say you were safer in a ship in Hong Kong harbour
than you were on land.'

Christy shuddered. 'I think I'd rather feel there

was solid earth under my feet.' She looked out over the calm, mirror-like surface of the water. 'I can cope when it's like this, but boats make me nervous.'

'Do they?' Brand sounded almost pleased. 'Then that's another lesson. Once I get the radio fixed, I'll take you out sailing in *Moondancer*.'

'That's your yacht, isn't it?'

'Well I'm not sure I'd call her a yacht. . .' He grinned. 'That conjures up something flashy and luxurious with a resident crew and less than thirty years old. So don't get your hopes up. Apart from a boat-boy who looks after her when she's in harbour, the crew consists of me, me and me. And any innocent maidens I can lure on board, of course. So is it a date?'

'I'm not sure. . .' It wasn't the thought of the sailing that scared her. Or at least, not most. It was the fact that, when he had said it, her first reaction had been one of pleasure.

'Nonsense; you'll enjoy it. I can take you. . .' Brand launched into a description of the beauties she would miss if she turned down his offer; the bays and islands only reachable by boat. And as she listened, Christy found her fears receding.

He was just a man, after all. . . His words seemed to recede into the background, leaving only his voice. A rich, deep voice, now brightened with pleasure in what was obviously his favourite subject.

'She's an old-fashioned deep-keeler, but with the spinnaker up and a fresh breeze she'll pick up her skirts no problem. . .' His hair flopped down over his forehead and he pushed it back. Christy watched in fascination as the black curls rippled between his fingers, still damp from the land's humid heat.

His words washed over her and she was vaguely aware that she hadn't the faintest idea what most of them meant. Spinnaker. . . Hadn't he said that was some kind of sail? Or had it been a rope? She couldn't remember.

But it didn't matter. What mattered was that for the first time she was seeing Brand Sutcliffe as a person; not as a client to be placated, nor a pirate to be feared. Not as a danger.

Just as a man.

And it came as a shock to realise how much she liked him.

It seemed like far less than an hour before the ferry sailed calmly through a network of what looked like huge dry stone walls, almost submerged in the blue water. But glancing at her watch, Christy found that Brand's estimate of their journey time had been correct to within five minutes.

'Doesn't time fly when you're enjoying yourself?'

He must have noticed her look of surprise, she thought wryly. Either that or he really could read her mind. . . She leant further out over the side of the boat so that he wouldn't see her face. 'What are those wall things, Brand?'

'Typhoon breakwaters. To protect the harbour.' He waved his hand around the small boats moored in clusters between the stone walls and the shore. 'These junks are home to their owners, not just transport. Even during typhoons.'

As the ferry sailed nearer, Christy saw what he meant. What she had taken for brightly coloured bunting on some of the boats was actually washing, hung up to dry in the breeze, and children were playing on deck as naturally as in any English back garden. 'But surely. . .' She twisted her neck to look back at the breakwater. 'Would that stop a typhoon? It doesn't look high enough. Surely the water would just go over the top?'

'That's true enough.' Brand nodded. 'It does. But it takes some of the force out of it first. A wall that was high enough to stop the sea would be smashed to pieces. The first thing to know about typhoons is that nothing will stop them. With a typhoon, you have to submit to survive.'

There was a note of respect in his voice that spoke of personal experience. 'Have you ever been caught by one?'

'At sea? Only once, when I was about fifteen. That was in a fishing junk. Never in *Moondancer*, though we've seen some pretty rough weather together. But I'm sure she'd come through it like a lady.'

He almost sounded as if he'd like to find out. Christy shivered. What must it be like to be trapped in one of those ramshackle boats at the mercy of the wind that could tear buildings from the ground?

Brand smiled at her anxious expression. 'Don't look so anxious, little rabbit. It's been a very quiet season this year. And if one did blow up, we'd get plenty of warning. With modern weather-forecasting techniques, there's no excuse for being caught out. You'll be safe enough.'

The ferry shuddered gently to a stop by the quay and he stood up, holding out a hand to steady her. 'Anyway, just to make sure, we'll have a word with Tin Hau while we're here.'

'Tin Hau?' There was something in the way he said the name that made it sound unmistakably feminine, and Christy felt a pang of something worryingly like jealousy as she followed him into the crush to disembark. 'Is she another of your. . .lady-friends?'

For some reason, Brand seemed to find that amusing. 'You could say that,' he agreed. 'I'll introduce you later. After lunch.'

The mention of food made Christy realise just how hungry she was. She had barely started her breakfast when Brand had interrupted it and the sea air of the journey across had stimulated her appetite.

'That sounds like a good idea.' They emerged from the semi-darkness of the ferry terminal and stood together on the quayside, blinking in the sudden brightness of the midday sun. Christy's stomach chose that moment to concur with a very unladylike rumble, and she laughed, feeling suddenly unreasonably happy. The sunlight poured through her like a stream of pure energy.

'I'm so hungry I could eat a horse. Even a Chinese horse.'

'Stir-fried with water-chestnuts? That comes later in the syllabus. This is just lesson two. For the moment, we'll stick to the easy stuff.' He started to walk along the quay towards a row of ramshackle corrugated iron shelters perched right on the edge of the harbour wall. 'Do you like fresh fish?'

'I love it.' A feeling of relief made her reply all the more fervent. Surely they couldn't do anything very awful to fresh fish. . .? But whatever happened, she was determined to eat it without complaint. Somehow, it seemed very important to show Brand she wasn't the timid little rabbit he thought her to be.

'Well you'll never have it fresher than this. Watch out—it's a bit wet underfoot.'

'Wet' was an understatement. Christy picked her way gingerly through what seemed to be a constant stream of water flowing across the pavement and found herself looking down at a row of shallow plastic trays. Hoses led into them and water spilled constantly over the top. That explained the wetness of the pavement.

But it wasn't what caught the eye. Moving languidly around in the tanks were fish of all imaginable—and several unimaginable—sizes and colours; from tiny angelfish, brilliant as jewels, to a four-foot monster in stone-grey that seemed to fix her with its malevolent stare. Lobsters waved their raffia-tied claws in a pantomime of threat or greeting and one small blue crab finally succeeded in its determined bid for freedom and scuttled madly towards the harbour wall.

It was a zoo; a living kaleidoscope of colour. But not until she saw the girl in charge pass Brand a water-filled bag which writhed and wriggled did Christy realise that it was also lunch.

The cook at the restaurant Brand had selected—if you could call a market stall with a charcoal-fired stove and four kitchen tables a restaurant—didn't seem surprised that his guests should bring the menu along with them.

Christy averted her eyes as the fish was expertly dispatched with a cleaver and rapidly cleaned, before being committed to a pan of almost unbelievable blackness. She spent the next ten minutes trying not to look too carefully at her surroundings. She had a feeling that they might not stand up to fastidious scrutiny.

'Good food never came out of a spotless kitchen,' Brand teased her cheerfully. 'Don't worry, I've been eating here for years.'

Then you've probably built up an immunity, she thought tartly. But her pride wouldn't let her voice her misgivings. And the food, when it arrived, was so delicious that it drove all other thoughts from her mind.

'I think you've been hiding your light under a bushel, young lady.' Brand leaned back at last with a sigh of repletion and took another sip of the fragrant, milkless tea which they had drunk throughout the meal. The remains of the fish, and the dishes of rice and vegetables that had accompanied it, lay demolished in the centre of the table.

'Where did a non-foreign-food-eating little rabbit like you learn to use chopsticks like that?'

Christy grinned, glad for once to be able to surprise him. 'Two terms at a finishing school in Switzerland,' she said smugly. 'Since as far as Madame was concerned we were all destined to be the wives of ambassadors, we were taught the art of coping gracefully with whatever cutlery was on offer. In fact

Chinese chopsticks are relatively easy—the Japanese version comes to a point at the end. Very tricky.'

'Finishing school?' He raised his eyebrows questioningly. 'I wouldn't have thought that was the normal route into a career in computers. And why only two terms? Did they run out of cutlery to teach you? Or did you disgrace yourself by eating peas with your knife?'

'Not exactly. . . My father took me away. Through a window in the middle of the night.' Christy giggled—then realised with surprise that she had never seen it as funny before. Certainly not at the time. . . 'The money had run out again, you see. Actually, two terms was quite good going. I worked out once that I'd been to sixteen schools.'

'Quite an exciting upbringing. What did—does—your father do?'

'Poppa?' Amazingly, it didn't hurt to talk. 'Oh, he's an entrepreneur; that's what it says in his passport. And quite a successful one—about forty-nine percent of the time. Unfortunately, however much money he makes, he always seems to lose it again.'

'A talent for snakes as well as ladders.'

She nodded, smiling. 'Yes, that describes it very well. I think the trouble is that when things are going well he gets bored; so he pulls his money out and puts it in something else. Usually something risky. It's like playing roulette; eventually, he's bound to lose. And then he's back to square one.'

'And asking you for money.'

'Yes, I——' Christy stopped in mid-sentence. 'How did you know that?'

'I didn't. But I guessed. The day you arrived, when you had your little weep, you were muttering something about someone trying to borrow money from you, and feeling guilty at turning them down. And then later you mentioned you'd seen your father just before you came out here. I'm right, aren't I? That's why you were so upset.'

There didn't seem to be any point denying it. 'I hate refusing him,' she said wistfully. 'Mum died when I was little, and Poppa's always relied on me. . . He really believes that he's offering me a wonderful opportunity and he can never undertand why I don't leap at the chance. But that flit from "Madame Bouillet's Establishment for Young Ladies" finished it for me. I swore I was never going to get involved again.'

'You left home?'

'I didn't have a home to leave—that had gone down with everything else. But I officially declared independence. I left school and got a job doing temporary secretarial work. That's when I acquired Sam, and the flat.' Christy smiled at the memory. 'One of the girls who shared it was going to Australia and couldn't take her cat with her. So I said I'd look after him—and somehow, when the others moved on, Sam and I just stayed.'

'So how did a temporary typist turn into a partner in a computer software house?' He looked at her with curiosity and Christy found herself wishing that her story were a bit more exciting than the truth.

'I took a temp. job with a big computer company—working for Mike, in fact. He was a project manager there. He just happened to be interviewing potential trainees and he left an aptitude test form lying round the office.'

Brand looked puzzled. 'A what?'

'It's a sort of quiz to find out if the applicants have the right sort of mind to succeed in computers,' she explained. 'I'd always liked puzzles, so I did it for fun one lunchtime and by accident it got marked along with the others.'

'And you passed?'

Christy nodded, smiling faintly as she remembered Mike's shocked reaction. 'I scored top marks, apparently. So Mike persuaded the company to take me on despite my lack of formal qualifications. I worked there for five years until the company moved out of London and Mike decided to set up on his own.'

'He asked you to go in with him? As a partner? I'm surprised you considered the idea.' Brand sounded pleased, as well as surprised. 'You weren't tempted to squirrel your redundancy money away in the building society and find another nice safe job working for someone else?'

Christy felt warmed by his approbation. It would be easy to keep quiet and bask in it, like a cat in the sun. But her natural honesty forced her to admit the truth. 'Well, actually, I'm not really his partner.'

'What? But he said——'

'Yes, I know.' She felt a momentary apprehension. Was she risking her professional credibility by her confession? But it was too late to draw back.

'Mike calls me that, because he thinks I ought to be,' she explained. 'We've been together from the start, and I've always been his second-in-command. He's always nagging at me to buy in as a full partner, but I've never wanted to be financially involved; I'm much happier just drawing a salary.' And squirrelling it away, she thought with a pang. Looked at through Brand's eyes, her way of life began to look as drab as her London-style clothes.

But he didn't seem as scornful of her sensible outlook as she had expected. 'Still, it can't have been an easy option, setting up a business from scratch. And Mike must rely on you a lot. . . You're not quite the rabbit you make yourself out to be, Christy— whatever you believe.'

She coloured slightly, uncomfortably aware of her pleasure at his approval—and of the fact that she had just told him more about herself than she had ever told anyone. Even Mike. . . What was there about Brand Sutcliffe that let him slip so easily through her defences?

She would have to be careful. But to her relief he made no attempt to probe deeper. After complimenting the cook and paying for the meal with what looked like a ridiculously small amount of money, he led her back along the quayside to a much smaller jetty than the one where the ferry had arrived.

Immediately there was a chorus of cries from the small boats tied up to the pier and harbour wall, as all the owners competed to gain their custom. The one Brand picked was already so crowded that Christy could hardly believe it was safe. In fact the woman in charge looked as if she would sink it on her own. Her round moon face was split by a grin-full of gold teeth and her flesh bulged exuberantly between the pale green bangles she wore on her massive arms.

With Oriental stoicism, the existing passengers shuffled even closer together to make room on the hard wooden bench for the two new arrivals. Christy found herself sitting between a woman carrying a live chicken in a bamboo basket and a man with a bowl of what looked horrifyingly like intestines bal-anced on his lap.

'Where are we going, Brand?' She had to fight not to show her disgust. 'Couldn't you have picked one of the others?'

Brand shook his head. 'We're just crossing the harbour to Sai Wan village; it won't take long. And if we'd have picked an empty *kaido* we'd have had to wait until it was as crowded as this before it would leave. Besides, I want you to see old Milly. She's quite a character. She's buried three husbands and she's as rich as Croesus. And she's never spent a night on land in her whole life.'

Christy watched as the huge woman started up the motor and released the little ferry from its mooring with surprising deftness for one so bulky. She didn't look rich. But by now she was past doubting what Brand Sutcliffe said. He had been right too often.

'You want me, Christy. . . That's lesson one. . .' A spirit of recklessness overtook her. He was right. She did want him. And perhaps it was time for the running to stop.

* * *

Brand was right, too, about the visit to Tin Hau. It was interesting. The little red and gold temple nestled in the cliffs above Sai Wan village, overlooking the harbour that was the goddess's special responsibility.

Copying the actions of the other worshippers, Christy carefuly planted her burning joss-sticks in the trough of sand before the altar and watched the curls of fragrant smoke coil upwards to Tin Hau's red and gold image. And as she followed her companion back out into the brilliantly contrasting sunshine, she remembered ruefully that she had been feeling jealous of the Queen of Heaven and Goddess of the Sea.

'One of my lady-friends indeed. . .' Brand's deep voice buzzed in her ear as they picked their way down the steep path which led to the beach. And for a moment, she was tempted to tell him the truth. To say, I was jealous. . .

The words hovered on her tongue, with all their dangerous, desirable implications. Three little words that would tear away the defences that she had so carefully constructed, the defences that now held her trapped. But her foot caught on a rock. She stumbled, and Brand caught her arm; his grip strong and matter-of-fact; his voice concerned.

'Are you OK? It's steep here. Let me go first.' Christy nodded, and let him move ahead. The moment was past, but the memory of it stayed with her, haunting her. What would he have done if she had spoken? Would he have stopped there, on the narrow path, and taken her into his arms? She remembered the softness of his lips on hers. Would he have kissed her again?

'For God's sake, Christy. . .' she muttered to herself. She felt light-headed and somehow detached, as if she had a fever. Perhaps it was sunstroke. . . She could see Brand just a few yards below her, the muscles of his shoulders moving with casual grace under the sweat-dampened cotton of his shirt. And a surge of physical desire rushed through her, with such strength that she was left gasping.

Once on the beach, Brand slipped off his clothes with a complete lack of self-consciousness, leaving only a brief pair of swimming shorts that he had been wearing underneath. Christy sent up a quick prayer of thanks that she had thought to do the same. As it was, her hands fumbled with the buttons on her skirt and shook as she pulled her cotton top over her head, acutely conscious of her near-nakedness—and of his admiring gaze.

'A true English pallor,' he teased. He was anything but pale. His body was a warm gold-brown, like antique pine. Or honey, Christy thought. Smooth golden honey, thick and luscious on the spoon. . . The dark hair that crinkled on his chest and legs was beaded with sweat and she had to fight back an insane urge to reach out and run her fingers through its roughness.

It must be the heat. . . Heat did affect people like that sometimes, didn't it? In the tropics? 'I think I'll go for a swim,' she stammered. Could he tell what was going on inside her head? Did it show?

But if it did, he gave no sign of noticing. 'Not yet,

I think.' He bent to rummage in the pocket of his jacket, pulling out a small plastic bottle of sun-cream which he tossed across to her. 'Give it another few minutes; and get some of that on quick.'

Obediently, she started to rub the warm cream into her skin, feeling his eyes follow her hands as they moved over her body. It was a strangely ritual sensation, as if she were anointing herself for sacrifice.

His voice broke into her thoughts with down-to-earth practicality. 'I'll do your back.'

'Oh, no—I can manage.' The protest came out with all the force of fear behind it. If he touched her. . . Christy wasn't sure what would happen then. But she had a feeling that something might explode.

'Don't be a fool.' He sounded irritated, and Christy realised that he had taken her words to mean that the old barriers between them were back in place. 'It may be hazy here, but that doesn't reduce the strength of the sun.' And before she could react he had taken the bottle back from her and was squirting cream on to the palm of his hand. 'Lie down so I can see what I'm doing. If I miss a patch you'll feel it tomorrow, I promise.'

But a little sunburn seemed a pale threat compared to what she was feeling now. His hands moved methodically over her back, sliding under the narrow straps of her bikini and smoothing round her shoulders and the curve of her waist. Her skin was on fire with his touch.

Oh, don't stop. She ground her fingers into the coarse, crystalline sand in the effort not to speak the words out loud. Pictures, images assailed her. If his hands slipped round to cup her breasts. . .

'Ow!' She started up, her bottom still stinging from the slap it had received. 'What was that for?'

'For enjoying it,' he said slyly, watching her face. 'That's not till lesson three. Pupils who read ahead of teacher will be punished.' He moved towards her and she stumbled away, laughing, towards the sea.

CHAPTER SIX

'So is this it? The pirate's cave?' Christy looked round in disappointment. After less than an hour on the beach, Brand had prodded her judiciously on the arm and pronounced her 'done', suggesting that they should explore the pirate's lair he had mentioned at the racing. Christy had been looking forward to it. She had always seen Brand as a pirate, after all; it would be interesting to see him in his natural habitat.

But now, after a tiring climb over boulders and rocks, there was nothing to see. Only the presence of a wrinkled old woman selling what looked like cans of drink, and some Chinese characters scrawled in blue paint on the rock face, differentiated this little alcove in the cliff from a thousand other shelters. You could hardly call it a cave. . .

'Not here. This is just the entrance. Down there.' He pointed at the rocky floor, just past where the old woman was squatting, and Christy followed his gesture in puzzlement.

'What do you mean? I can't see anything.'

'Of course not. That's why Cheung Po Tsai chose it as his refuge. You could walk right past it and never know that it was there. Have another look.'

Christy gingerly approached the area he had indicated, half expecting the ground to open up mysteriously beneath her. As she passed the old woman, she saw that her wares were not drinks but torches. For hire, presumably. So there must be something to see. . .

But there was nothing. Behind her, she could heard Brand bargaining over the torches, but even his fluent Cantonese made no impression. Implacable in the knowledge of her unassailable market position, the old woman's cracked voice reiterated her first extortionate price.

'Five dollar!'

Christy smiled. Not long ago she would have been irritated by such blatant profiteering. Now it was beginning to seem all part of the Hong Kong character. Just so long as there really was a cave.

Then, stepping from one rock to another, she was suddenly aware of a cool breeze on her legs. Coming from below. But looking down eagerly, she realised that it was coming from the merest gap between two rocks. Much too small for an entrance. . .

'I see you've found it.' Brand came up from behind and handed her a battered old torch. 'Well hidden, isn't it? Old Po Tsai knew what he was doing. And feel the breeze; the air is always fresh. With a good stock of food and a few barrels of water, he could have gone to ground here for weeks.'

He sounded positively enthusiastic, Christy thought, following his gaze. Perhaps he really was a pirate at heart. . .

'Mind you——' he shook his torch and the light flickered off and then on '—I think he would have had to go for the ten-dollar lighting.'

But Christy was hardly listening to what he was

saying. She was staring aghast at the dark gap between the rocks at her feet.

'You mean that's it?' She looked up in horror and saw him grin in confirmation. 'That—crack? I couldn't possibly get through there.'

'Well, if I can, I'm sure you ought to be able to make it. It's bigger than it looks.' And with no further discussion, he tucked his still-lighted torch in his belt and sat down on the rock with his legs dangling through the slim gap. 'See you inside.'

With one smooth wriggle, he was gone. And even though Christy knew exactly where he was, buried in the rocks beneath her feet, the speed of his disappearance sent an eerie shiver down her spine. It was as if he had been spirited away. . .

'Come on, little rabbit—I'd have thought burrowing was just your line.' The disembodied voice was joined by an equally disembodied hand, beckoning with crooked finger from the crack in the rocks. 'Just sit down and slide through. There's no drop to speak of—and anyway, I'll be here to catch you.'

'I can't, Brand. . .'

'Trust me.'

The voice that echoed hollowly from the cave sounded ominous, like the voice of some pagan god. And suddenly, it seemed to Christy that there was more here at stake than just a bit of sightseeing. That she was standing at a crossroads and this was a test, a challenge. And one that she didn't dare fail.

Gritting her teeth, she copied what Brand had done, sitting on the edge of that dreadful dark hole and dangling her legs into nothingness. Her hand closed convulsively on the torch. Then, before she could lose her nerve, she slid precipitately forward, stifling a scream of mixed fear and relief as she felt his arms close round her waist and draw her downwards into the dark.

Brand's torch flickered and went out. And when Christy fumbled in panicky haste to switch hers on, she was rewarded with nothing more illuminating than a dull click.

'Brand!'

'Calm down, little rabbit. You're doing very well. Now just sit there a minute while I fix these, will you?' She could feel his teasing grin like a warm glow in the dark, reassuring her. Gently, he lowered her down on to the dry, surprisingly smooth, cave floor. 'Don't go rushing off, now.'

In the darkness, all her senses seemed to have become more acute. As Brand fiddled with the torches, she could hear the slightest sound with pin-sharp clarity; even the tiny musical jingle as he shook one of the bulbs close to his ear.

'The filament's gone on that one,' he said, confirming what she had already guessed. 'I'll go up and change it.'

'No!' At the thought of being left alone in the cave, even for a few minutes, Christy felt the panic rise again. And she knew that if she accompanied him back to ground level, nothing would make her abandon herself to that dark hole again. It was now or never.

'What about the other torch? Can't you fix that?'

'I'm not sure.' There were more small sounds and

then a sickly flicker of light. 'That's the best I can do, I think. But there seems to be a loose connection. It might go out again.'

'Not if we're careful.' Now that she could see her surroundings, Christy felt a sense of adventure rear its cautious head somewhere inside her. She was sitting on the floor of a small, round cavern about six feet across. A fall of boulders, forming a natural stairway into the cave, pressed into her back and she could feel the breeze she had felt on the surface blowing past her to the almost invisible entrance above.

Beside her squatted Brand, holding the torch.

'It's not very big, is it? Were they very small pirates?'

'Idiot,' he said affectionately. 'It was only an emergency bolthole—and besides, this isn't the whole of it.' He flashed the torch over the far wall, and Christy saw a black archway leading off into a darkness too dense for the torchlight to penetrate. 'But I thought I'd let you get your breath back first. There's another drop down to get to the tunnel—I'll go first, then I can help you down.'

Now that she looked, Christy could see where the floor dropped away. But what lay beyond was swathed in shadows. She felt her sense of adventure take a pace or two back and knew that if she didn't act swiftly she would lose her courage.

'Come on, then.' She stood up carefully to avoid bumping her head on the low sloping roof. 'Let's get on with it.' She felt quite proud of her voice, all considered. It was hardly shaking at all.

Brand grinned at her in the flickering light with an affectionate query in his expression that suggested she hadn't fooled him by her show of confidence. He beckoned her over to the edge of the drop and she followed nervously.

'You take the torch while I jump down.' Christy took it, and for a moment their fingers touched. She shivered at the buzz of sensation that passed between them and knew instinctively that he felt it too. . . Her breathing quickened. And the fear inside her turned into a very different kind of tension.

A wanting; a hunger. 'You want me, Christy. . . That's lesson one.' Taking the torch, she trained it on the ground. She didn't dare to look him in the eyes.

Steadying himself casually with one hand on the edge, Brand jumped down the six-foot drop as if he were stepping off a kerb. He landed like a cat, noiselessly.

'You next.' He held out his arms to catch her and Christy leaned down to grasp his shoulders firmly. The muscles of his neck were taut beneath her hands.

'Ready?'

Christy braced herself. But just as she made the leap, a booming crash echoed through the silence of the cave, as if the pirate's refuge was once more under siege.

'Oh!' She half jumped, half fell into Brand's waiting arms and the torch flew from her hand. It hit the floor and rolled away towards the tunnel with an ominous jangling sound.

'What was that?'

'Only thunder. I thought the weather might break. Listen.'

She strained her ears and heard, muffled through the stone walls, the soft patter-patter of rain falling on the rocks above.

'It's raining!' Stories she had heard of caves turning to underground streams came jostling back into her mind. 'Is it safe? Shouldn't we go back up?'

'And get soaked to the skin? No; we're better off where we are. These storms don't last very long.'

'But I've broken the torch. . .' Her voice petered out. His arms were still around her, holding her close. And she was suddenly overwhelmingly, unbearably conscious of his closeness; of the warmth that radiated from his body; of the salt, musky smell of his skin.

'I don't need a torch to see you by, Christy,' he whispered unsteadily.

She tried to pull back, but the rough stone wall was behind her, blocking her escape. And then the moment of panic was over. The fear turned to a trembling excitement. And she realised that she didn't want to escape at all.

She felt his hands go gently to her face, one rough palm cradling her chin as his fingers caressed her. 'My hands can see you.' He traced the curve of her nose; the line of her lips. 'I don't need a five-dollar torch to tell me you're beautiful.'

Wonderingly, her own hand reached to his face, caressing the warm, moist smoothness of his forehead, beaded with sweat in the heavy heat, and the rough male contrast of his chin. Her fingers traced

his cheekbone, feeling with preternatural sensitivity
the silky texture of the scar which might so easily
have plunged him into darkness for ever. . .

She touched his lips. And felt the softness of his
tongue and the hard sharpness of his teeth as he
nipped playfully at her fingers, drawing them into
the warmth of his mouth and delicately sucking in
turn each sensitive tip. Five separate tendrils of erotic
sensation crept down her arm and twined like ivy
around her spine, constricting her breath and making
her shudder with pleasure.

Blindly, she moved her body against him, deeper
and deeper into his embrace. And heard her own
voice whisper his name.

'Brand. . .' And then his lips were seeking hers in
the darkness, claiming them, sealing them to silence.
And all fear, all shame, had gone. The dark lay across
them like a kindly cloak, drawing them together in
its velvet folds. There was nothing but the warmth of
his mouth and the pressure of his body against her.
And the compelling desire that wove its web between
them. Nothing in the world. . .

His lips held her captive as he caressed her body,
moulding its shape with scarce-controlled urgency,
as if to memorise every contour. His touch left a path
of fire in her flesh. And then his hands—she caught
her breath as those strong, gentle, rope-roughened
pirate's hands slipped under the silk of her top to
capture the cool softness of her breasts. Teasing
them; soothing them. Possessing them. And feeding
the flame of desire that burned within her.

Her body was melting, melting in the heat of it;

turning to liquid pleasure at the sensual promise of his touch.

'Touch me, Christy.' His voice was almost a groan. And now it was her turn to explore his body, her hands kneading the taut muscles of his back and buttocks, drawing him ever closer to her in the kindly darkness.

All thought, all consciousness, all will was gone. And there was only the harsh touch of the rock behind her, and the feel of him, and the hardness of him pressing against her. And the burning in the depths of her that drove her on.

His hands came up to twist deep into her hair, straining her head back against the rock to expose her throat to his mouth. But his watch caught fast, tugging the roots so that she yelped with pain, and the heavy chained gold strap fell loosely around his wrist.

'Hell.' Brand's arm came across her as he struggled one-handed to replace the catch, the gold chain tapping against the rock by her ear. In the darkness, the sound was unnaturally loud. Like a warning.

But the sound that Christy heard inside her head was of another gold chain—tapping, tapping. The chain that Brand had given Rainbow; his 'thank-you' for the night they had spent together.

And with the sound, her sense of self-preservation came flooding back. What was she doing to risk this sort of involvement with a man who was almost certainly seeing another woman? If she hadn't come to her senses. . .

'Brand—we ought to go. Someone else might

come.' She tried to wriggle from the cage his arms made around her, but there was no escape.

'Don't worry, Christy.' His voice was soft and muffled with desire. 'No one will come. Not in a rainstorm. And the old woman will have gone to find shelter. We're all alone. And this is the last lesson, little rabbit. The one where we make love. . .

He bent to kiss her again, his lips grazing her mouth. But with sudden violence she wrenched herself free. 'No, Brand—I can't—you mustn't.'

'Mustn't I?' She could feel him struggle with the tension in his voice. 'What's the matter, Christy?' he whispered more gently. 'Why are you afraid?'

But she had no defence left but the truth. 'Because we're not—you don't love me, Brand.' There; it was out now, and as if a dam had broken the words started to tumble out in incoherent explanation. 'I do want you; you know that and I'm not denying it. But it's not enough. I—I'm not like Rainbow. I couldn't have an affair with you out here and then go home and forget all about it. If there were anything else; anything more. . . But there isn't; there can't be. It's too risky. We live in different worlds. . . I have to think of my future, Brand, my security. You have to understand.'

'Oh, I think I understand.' There was a dangerous edge to his voice that made her shiver with fear. 'You've let me feel the merchandise so now you flash the price-tag, is that it? You sneer at Rainbow, but at least she's honest about what she wants.' His words cut her like a whip. 'What are you after, Christy? Marriage? Or just a nice little addition to that building society account? If it's marriage, you can forget it. It's a long time since I was stupid enough to pay for my pleasures in anything but cash.'

Reaching out in the darkness, he pulled her back against him, running a hand with deliberate crudeness up her thigh to where the warm moisture of her arousal waited to betray her. 'What if your price is too high, Christy? What if I decide not to pay?'

Christy forced herself not to struggle. 'Don't. Please.' There was a long silence. The atmosphere in the cave seemed almost electric with tension. 'That wasn't what I meant, Brand. Honestly.'

For a moment his muscles seemed to lock into rigidity; his fingers biting into her arm. And then, with a shuddering sigh, he let her skirt fall back around her shaking legs. 'No, I know you didn't, I suppose.' He sounded infinitely weary. 'I know what you want. You want guarantees, don't you, Christy? You want a nice safe husband and a joint bank account and two point four nice safe children. And you're afraid I would jeopardise that.' He paused. 'You're a virgin, aren't you?' He didn't wait for her to confirm or deny. 'I don't think you know what loving is.'

But I love you. . . The darkness hid the lightning flash of realisation that zig-zagged through her at his words. She was in love with Brand. It was impossible—ridiculous. But it was true. And she knew at once that he must never know.

'Is it so obvious?' She hardly knew what she was saying. But his answer was like a dagger in her heart.

'Loving means taking risks, Christy—at any level.

Even the most casual. And you've never taken a risk in your whole life.'

He said goodbye at the door of her room. The journey back had been one of awkwardness and constrained silence, with Christy twisting uncomfortably in her seat and painfully aware of the mud-stained condition of her clothes. Only now did the atmosphere seem to thaw a little.

'Christy——'

'Yes?' She turned back eagerly from her efforts with the key.

'I enjoyed today.'

'So did I.'

'Then isn't that enough?' Brand seemed to search for the words to express his meaning. 'Why can't you just enjoy what we have, Christy? You like me, you want me—and I feel the same. There's something special between us, something that's too precious to throw away.'

He hurried on as if to prevent interruption. 'I can't claim to love you, but I do care about you, Christy. I wouldn't hurt you. We'd be good together, I know we would.'

She opened her mouth to speak, but he shook his head. 'Think about it, Christy. Do you want to stay a rabbit all your life? Now kiss me goodnight.'

Dumbly she held up her face for him to kiss; but what had started as a chaste touch ended with a searching embrace that left her trembling.

'That's your homework, little one. Remember to want me.' For a moment his gaze flickered and she saw a glimpse of an intensity behind his words. And then he turned and strode off down the long corridor.

Christy watched him until he disappeared, seeing as if in slow motion the way his shoulders moved in rhythm with his steps, the way his arms swung with loose assurance by his sides. She was reminded of the first time she had seen him, in the airport. There was a solidity about him; she had noticed it at once. An air of being very much physically *there*.

His absence seemed to leave a yawning gap, and for a moment she was seized with the impulse to run after him and ask him to stay. But instead she closed the door quietly behind her and started to strip, throwing her clothes into a hotel laundry-bag for collection. Her hands strayed for a moment over the soft contours of her own skin.

It felt different, somehow. Alive; awakened. More sensitive. . . Christy felt a warm knot of desire twist inside her. 'Remember to want me. . .' Well, there would be no problem with that. She'd learned her lesson well.

Too well. What was it he had said to her? 'You don't know what love is. . .' And she had let him think it was true.

But that was the other lesson Brand Sutcliffe had taught her. She had learned to love him. And it was likely to be the most painful lesson of her life.

The room was dark except for the glow of the clock by her bedside and Christy's breathing was deep and even. But sleep itself proved elusive. After the day's

unaccustomed exercise, her body ached with tiredness, but her rebellious mind spun off in exhilarated
spirals that she was powerless to check—and terrified to follow to their logical conclusion.

She had tried to push out of her mind the new self-
knowledge that had welled up in the darkness of the
cave, but now, in this new darkness, it came clam-
ouring back. I love him. . . It couldn't be true.

She knew so little about Brand Sutcliffe—except
that their lives were miles apart. And he had made it
painfully clear that there were limits to their involvement—limits that she knew would tear her apart.
And yet. . .

Looking at it coldly, Christy knew that she was a
fool not to put him out of her mind, whatever the
cost. But there had been nothing cold about the way
he had held her in his arms; nothing cold about the
way he had kissed her, touched her. . . And there
was nothing cold now about the fever of frustration
that denied her her sleep.

Was she a fool, as he said, to reject the idea of a
brief affair? The arguments buzzed round and round
in Christy's head. Perhaps it would hurt less, in the
inevitable future when she returned to England, if
she at least had her memories to look back on. Or
would that just stamp his image irrevocably into her
flesh?

She was standing at a cliff-edge and he was on the
beach and asking her to step off into the void to join
him. 'No guarantees. . .' But if she turned aside she
might lose him for ever.

And there was Rainbow. . . But somehow, the

thought of the Chinese girl no longer filled her with the twisting jealousy that she had felt earlier. The more she thought about it, the more she knew that Brand hadn't talked or acted like a man who was involved elsewhere. . .

There was the bracelet. But Christy found herself wondering if the much vaunted present might have been a parting, rather than a thank you, gift. Her mind seized eagerly on this explanation, testing it and giving it substance.

It would make sense. After all, however wealthy he was, Brand could hardly be in the habit of rewarding his mistress so richly for every night of love. Whereas if he had just said goodbye. . .

If only it were true. Christy felt that she could have forgiven Brand any number of past mistresses if only he would return her feelings now. Except that he didn't know what those feelings were. And she had no intention of enlightening him.

The debate swung round full circle, battling it out inside her head. The glowing figures of the clock showed the minutes turn into hours as she tossed and turned in the wide, empty bed, the once cool sheets now tangled and dampened with sweat.

Until at last she gave up trying. At three o'clock she reached for the phone and put through a call to England, calculating that the time difference should let her catch Mike at home.

'Christy!'

Mike's voice was so clear that she could have been back in England, ringing from the flat. But to her own surprise, that fleeting image brought no home-sickness in its wake. I've crossed the Rubicon, she thought, with a mixture of fear and excitement. I'm enjoying myself—I've let him get to me. God knows what happens now. . .

At the other end of the line, Mike had obviously been doing a few calculations. 'What on earth are you doing phoning me at this time?' he went on. 'It must be the middle of the night over there. Is something wrong with the system?'

Christy smiled to herself. Trust her boss to jump to the worst possible conclusion. 'I couldn't sleep,' she said soothingly. 'And don't worry, not because of work. It's all going pretty well so far. There's a lot to do, but if the suppliers deliver the equipment on time then there's no reason why we shouldn't make the deadline.'

'Then what's the problem? Don't tell me you're still jet-lagged? I told you; the only way round it is to force yourself to——'

'I'm not jet-lagged, Mike. There's nothing wrong. I just happened to be awake and so I thought I'd ring and see how you and Carol were keeping. And besides, there's something you can do for me.' Though you're not going to like it, she thought wryly. 'I want you to find out about quarantine regulations.'

'Carol and I are fine, Christy, but I'm not so sure about you. You sound—different somehow. Have you been drinking? Why the hell do you want to know about quarantine regulations at three o'clock in the morning?'

'Because I've found a cat.' As she spoke, Christy was uncomfortably aware how impractical her plan sounded. And how much Brand would disapprove. . . But I don't care, she told herself rebelliously. I *won't* leave him to starve or get run over or die of some horrible disease. And anyway, Brand won't know.

'A cat? Christy, is this a bad line? There are cats in England, you know. It isn't necessary to import them. In fact, I'm not even sure it's legal.'

'Well, this is a Chinese cat. Called Mauw. And I want to bring it back with me. Look, I know you'll think it's a stupid——'

'You're right, Christy, I do. Have you any idea——?'

'—but I'm not asking you, Mike. Just find out the rules, will you? Or do I have to run up the company phone-bill ringing Customs and Excise or whoever it is from here?'

Mike muttered something that might have been a reluctant assent. There was a slight pause, and then he spoke again. 'I've just realised what's different about you,' he said suspiciously. 'You sound *happy*. What's up? Is it just the thought of another term of servitude to some undeserving feline?'

'Well, not entirely.' She paused, not quite sure how to go on. 'I've been letting Brand Sutcliffe show me the sights of Hong Kong.'

'I see. . .' There was a wealth of meaning in that little word, 'see'. 'And?'

'And—he's very nice.' What an inadequate description that was. Like calling one of his precious typhoons 'a bit of a blow'. 'I like him a lot, Mike. And before you ask; yes, I am trying to keep my feet on the ground And yes, I probably will get hurt. And yes, I do think it's worth it. So don't grudge me the cat, OK? I might be in need of a bit of feline comfort when I get home.'

Listening to the stunned silence at the other end of the phone, Christy suddenly felt light-hearted, as if a weight had lifted from her mind. Somehow the decision had made itself. And she was right; it would be worth it. Whatever happened. Whatever the hurt. . .

'Poor Mike.' She found herself gurgling with laughter. 'I didn't mean to hit you with the whole lot like that. Are you still there?'

'Yes. . . I'm still here. And I think you're doing the right thing, kid. If you knew how much I've wanted to see you kick over the traces now and again. . . But do try to keep an anchor in somewhere, won't you? I'd hate you to hit the ground too hard.' The concern in his voice made her smile. But there was pride too. 'And Christy. . .' Mike seemed to be weighing up a decision. 'About this partnership thing. I was going to leave it until you got back, but since you seem to be coming out of your shell at last, maybe I'll mention it now. Only I do need someone to share the load, and if you're really not interested then I'll have to start bringing up one of the others. . . Give it a thought, will you?'

'OK, Mike. I'll think it over.' And as they brought the phone-call to an end, Christy realised that, this time, she might just say 'yes'.

* * *

How she survived the crazy weeks that followed, Christy would never understand. Always a firm believer in the old 'early to bed' adage, in England she had confined her social life largely to weekends. So, after spending her days in a frantic struggle to meet Brand's near-impossible deadline, by nightfall she should have been totally exhausted, ready only for sleep.

Only it didn't seem to work like that. A few weeks earlier, if anyone had told her that she would be shrugging off her tiredness to sample the restaurants and nightlife of Hong Kong, she would have thought they were raving—but Brand's company seemed to give her an energy and enthusiasm she had never suspected she might possess.

Two or three evenings a week, he would pick her up from her hotel and they would venture out into the spinning kaleidoscope of noise and light and colour that was the territory at night. Christy had moved a long way from her initial revulsion. She was beginning to realise that, beneath the bustle and confusion, Hong Kong had a vitality that was unlike anywhere else in the world.

It should have been idyllic. But it didn't help that, as her relationship with Brand developed, so Rainbow returned to her attitude of hostile and scarcely veiled insolence. She worked well and efficiently, but never missed a chance to make a poisoned remark.

And there was Mauw, too; now pronounced fit by the vet and released into Christy's custody. Unknown to Brand, she had arranged with the hotel to board him and Mike was—although reluctantly—

making the import and quarantine arrangements from his end.

But the little cat wasn't happy. Whenever she visited him in his cramped quarters in the basement of the hotel, he seemed to Christy to have shrunk further into his cage. He welcomed her affectionately, but there was a hopeless look in his eyes. Like a prisoner on visiting day, he knew that her kindness was only an interlude. And when she left, he no longer bothered to yowl.

Christy wished she could discuss it with Brand. But she knew what his solution would be—and besides, Brand himself was another of her problems. And one that seemed even more difficult to solve.

Despite the time they spent together, it seemed to Christy that they never recaptured the intimacy of the day in Cheung Chow. There was a constraint between them that hadn't been there before.

Brand seemed oddly distant. He would ignore her for days and then turn up in the lobby to take her out, acting sometimes as if he didn't even want to be there. She came to dread what she thought of as his 'black moods', when he seemed to take an almost sadistic pleasure in treating her harshly, as if trying to drive her away.

At times like those, Christy despised herself for not standing up to him. She should have slammed the door, refused to see him. . . But the hunger for his presence was too strong and she would follow him meekly to the Rolls, praying that the meal or the show would please him and be enough to change his mood.

And yet there were other times when he treated her with a tenderness that touched her heart; when they would dance and laugh and hold hands over the table in restaurants. Those were the times she came closest to happiness. But even then, there was something missing.

Christy knew what it was. They still hadn't made love, and it left a yawning gap in the centre of their relationship, like an open well in the middle of a room. They skirted carefully around the sides, saying nothing and pretending it didn't exist.

But its presence inhibited them. And Christy didn't know how to bridge it. Every night, when he took her home, she tried to nerve herself to make the first move. If he had escorted her to her room, as he had that first time, it might have been easier. He would have kissed her properly then, and that might have given her courage.

But as it was, they said goodbye in the lobby, his mouth just skimming her lips. And in that hurried, impersonal atmosphere, how could she say it? 'Come with me, Brand.' 'Let's go to bed.' 'Don't leave me.'

If he had given her even the slightest help. . . But he didn't, and she thought she understood why not. It had to be her decision. But it was so hard. . . And time was slipping away.

Tonight was one of the good nights. The computer system was finally installed and Christy had spent a long day trying to train a team of four clerical staff to feed it with the information about Brand's business that it would need to run.

It would have been a straightforward task if they had all spoken English. But as it was, every instruction had had to be fed through Rainbow—and at times the confusion that resulted had put Christy in mind of the old parlour-game, Chinese Whispers.

It was appropriate enough; and tomorrow would no doubt be the same. Yet here she was, looking out across the harbour from a roof-top restaurant high above the city—and enjoying every moment.

'You really don't have to entertain me every night,' she said half teasingly to her companion as they dropped back into their seats after a dance that had left her flushed and exhilarated. 'I'm sure you don't normally treat your suppliers like this.'

'Since most of them are male, I doubt if they would appreciate being taken dancing. And besides, they're not as pretty as you.' Brand ran his fingers along the length of her forearm, touching off a million tiny jolts of electricity that made her shiver with pleasure. 'You know I want to see you, Christy. Stop fishing for compliments.

For a moment, his accusation nudged her into seriousness. 'I just thought. . .' Despite his seeming enjoyment of their evening together, there was a brittleness to his mood, a tenseness below the surface that made it obvious that he had a lot on his mind. 'You must be busy at the moment, with only a week to go before the reception. I'd quite understand if you didn't have time to——'

'Look, Christy, if it didn't suit me to see you then, believe me, I wouldn't be here.' The edge of roughness to his voice made her pull back, hurt.

It was true, of course. She had been a fool to think that he might be so absorbed with her that he would forget his responsibilities. But did he have to make it quite so clear just what his priorities were?

But before she could speak he reached out for her hand across the table, softening his words with a smile that melted the hurt like a splinter of ice held in a warm hand. 'You're the best relaxation I could have, Christy. And besides, you won't see much more of me before next Saturday. Some of my backers are getting nervous; I may have to go away for a few days. So I'll be relying on you.'

Christy felt a surge of pleasure at his confidence. 'I actually think we're going to do it, Brand,' she glowed. 'Most of the equipment was installed yesterday, and the rest arrived tomorrow, including the computer terminal you wanted installed at your home.' A thought suddenly struck her. 'Oh—there will be someone there to let them in, will there? I'm sorry, I should have thought——'

But Brand only looked amused. 'That's not a problem.'

Of course; no doubt he would have a full-time *amah* at least; and probably other staff. The reminder of the differences between them gave her a momentary jolt, and she seemed to see their lives as two stubborn pieces of a jigsaw puzzle, refusing to mesh. . .

Resolutely, she pushed the thought away with a discipline that had become almost automatic. What had she said to Mike? That whatever happened, it would be worth it. She had gone into the relationship with her eyes open, knowing that there could be no real future for them together. That these few weeks might be all they ever had.

'So it's almost finished?'

For a moment, she thought he had read her mind, and felt her heart thump painfully. But he was still talking about work. . . She pinned a smile to her face, then felt it melt into naturalness as she started to tell him about her day. She had been right. The present was too precious to spoil by worrying. And the future might never come. . .

'We're getting there.' Her professional instincts told her it was time to sound a note of caution. 'The biggest hurdle is transferring all the information from your current filing systems on to the computer. It's a mammoth task—but a computer system is useless without data.'

'You think you can do it, though?' Christy nodded, surprised by the real anxiety in his voice. Although she knew he was planning to make the new system the centrepiece of his reception, it still took her aback that he laid so much emphasis on meeting the *Fung Shui* expert's deadline. It was so alien. . .and yet Brand, whether he believed it or not, treated it as matter-of-factly as an application for planning permission.

'And Rainbow's giving you all the help you need?' he went on. 'No communication problem?'

'Well, no, not really. . .' Christy decided not to mention the Chinese Whispers. There was nothing she could put her finger on, and probably they were as much her own fault as the Chinese girl's. 'She's been very efficient. And she's very keen to learn. This afternoon, I found her poring over the technical manuals and this evening, after we'd finished, she was experimenting with the system.'

'This evening?' Brand looked surprised. 'That doesn't sound like Rainbow—normally nothing comes between her and her social life. I have to wave a fat bonus at her to get her to stay a minute past half-past five. Maybe computers are less boring than I thought.'

'Well, she was still there when I left.' For some reason, the memory of Rainbow's delicate fingers, stabbing at the keys with blood-red nails, was obscurely unsettling. But there really wasn't any logical reason for her continued discomfort in dealings with the other girl, and Christy knew it would be unfair to draw such a nebulous feeling to Brand's attention.

The hostility that shimmered between them was understandable enough, after all. Working with a man as attractive as Brand Sutcliffe, it must have been seductively easy to fall into the trap of personal possessiveness. And Brand had obviously encouraged her.

A surge of pity overwhelmed her irrational dislike. Poor Rainbow. Whereas she was so lucky. . .

The Filipino band slid into a slow, romantic number and Brand stood up, holding out a hand in invitation and looking down at her with that smile that turned her bones to bubbles of champagne. Far below them in the harbour, silent boats moved slowly through a fairyland of lights. And then his arms were around her and the long notes of the saxophone filled her head as they moved together, dancing as though one heart, one mind propelled them.

Nestled against the strong wall of his chest, Christy felt a deep sense of security pervade her, her worries melting away. He did care; she could feel it in the way he held her and the way he looked at her. Whatever happened, they had had this.

He might not say it but she could see it in his eyes. I love you. . . And her own heart gave back the words she didn't dare to speak.

CHAPTER SEVEN

'So THIS is it, Mauw. Decision time. For both of us.'

Mauw gazed up at her with an almond-eyed look of intelligence that almost convinced Christy that her words had been understood. Sam had looked like that too; that was how she had got into the habit of feline conversations. There was a rap on the door, and she jumped, guiltily, assailed by a fleeting vision of Brand's reaction if he were to catch her talking to a cat. . .

But it was only room-service, with the pot of tea she had ordered. Once more alone, Christy took a few sips to calm her nerves. Then, positioning herself carefully in front of the mirror, she started to roll the pure silk stockings carefully up her legs squinting behind to check the straightness of the seams.

Thank goodness she had remembered at the last moment that the silk of her dress would cling to nylon. . . What else had she forgotten? It was all such a rush. But at least her dress was pressed and ready and the bag with her night-things packed. . .

Her mind ran on, preoccupied with the small practical minutiae of her preparations, as if to block out the real significance of that little airline bag. It lay on the bed, its scuffed exterior hardly impressive enough for such a potent symbol. Inside was a toothbrush, a change of clothes—and a silk night-dress that had taken her a whole afternoon to select from the lingerie department of one of Hong Kong's most luxurious stores.

It wasn't really a piece of luggage, thought Christy, as her eyes were drawn inexorably back to it. It was a burning boat. . .

Her new room-mate stretched out an explorative paw towards her leg and she dodged quickly out of reach. 'None of that. You've already made me late, you wicked animal. Why did you have to make such a fuss about getting into your nice basket? Anyone would think you didn't want to go free.'

Mauw dug his claws into the bedcover and stretched luxuriously, uttering a strange yowling noise that sounded very much like a complaint.

Christy reached down to tickle his tummy. 'Oh, Mauw, I will miss you. But you wouldn't have liked it in England, would you, darling? I should have realised that before. And you'll be much happier where I'm taking you. There's lots of birds and mice for you to catch, and no one to kick you or throw stones.'

The idea had occurred to her quite suddenly the previous day, when she had had to visit Brand's home on the Peak to install his computer terminal. True to his prediction, Brand himself had been away for most of the week, so after her work was finished she had been free to wander at liberty through the house and grounds.

It had been both more and less intimidating than she expected. More because, even as a newcomer, she couldn't help realising just how valuable such a property would be worth, set as it was in the territory's most sought-after district. But less because, despite its size and grandeur and the fact that many of the rooms were obviously never used for everyday living, the house was still somehow a home.

But the idea had come when the wizened little *amah*, determined to display the full glories of her domain, had taken Christy out to the grounds. There the manicured perfection of the lawns gave way beyond to a luxuriant tangle of jungly trees that faded into the woods which covered the top of the Peak.

Birds twittered in the branches and the scene could have been a thousand miles away from the concrete bustle of central Hong Kong. It was a cat's paradise. And Christy had thought immediately of Mauw.

She had been gradually coming to the realisation that the little cat would never settle happily into the life she had envisaged for him in England—even if his independent spirit survived the long months of quarantine before he could join her. He was as different from placid old Sam as if he had been another species.

But the problem had remained, what to do? She couldn't bear the thought of simply releasing him back into the hostile and dangerous environment where she had found him. The Peak's luxuriant woods seemed to be the ideal solution.

The little cat started to purr, as if he knew she was thinking about him. Christy smiled. 'There's a good puss. And now you have to go back in your basket.

Brand's car is coming to collect us in ten minutes, and I can't put my dress on with your claws flashing around. So please don't give me any trouble. . .'

She felt a flicker of unease. The cat which had looked so quiet and dejected in its cage at the basement kennels seemed to have grown considerably once restored to tail-swishing freedom.

But as if he sensed that, this time, the basket was just a stepping stone to a greater freedom, Mauw let himself be incarcerated without a murmur. He even licked Christy's hand through the wickerwork bars, his small rough tongue like living sandpaper on her skin.

So now it was her turn. Christy glanced across to where the black silk creation was hanging ready by the mirror, its sophisticated elegance mocking her nervousness. Could she really carry it off? Still, at least the rush meant she wouldn't have time for second thoughts. . .

Grabbing her make-up bag from the dresser, she gave Mauw a last scratch between the ears. 'Wish us both luck, puss,' she murmured. And his orange eyes blinked slowly in reply.

Christy let the chauffeur assist her from the back seat of the Rolls, realising for the first time that, dressed as she was, the courtesy was more than an empty gesture. The black silk fitted her like a second skin almost to the knees and required a certain care and attention to movement. She was uncomfortably aware that without that impassive helping hand her exit from the car would have been more floundering than elegant.

It was not an everyday dress. But from the moment of stunned and totally unselfconscious admiration when she had slipped it on in the hotel bedroom, and caught sight of herself in the mirror, Christy would have forgiven it anything.

The dress was undoubtedly beautiful. But more than that, it was absolutely and uniquely right. It was *her* dress—and the Christy who had looked back at her from the mirror had been a woman transformed, serenely confident in her own beauty.

Remembering that momentary vision, Christy felt something stir deep inside. A pulse of hope. Perhaps it wasn't impossible after all. Perhaps worlds could meet. Perhaps tonight. . .

But an impatient yowl from the back seat reminded her that it wasn't only her own future that hung in the balance. Reaching back into the plush interior of the Rolls, she lifted out the little cat's basket and carried it unsteadily around to the side of the house.

She could see the dark shapes of the trees silhouetted against the warm night sky and hear small scufflings in the bushes. Mauw could hear them too. As Christy bent down to unfasten the straps of his cage, she could feel his body tense with excitement.

The door fell open. But instead of dashing for freedom as she expected, the little cat walked delicately out on to the gravel and wound himself twice round her legs.

'Goodbye, Mauw,' she whispered. Her eyes were full of tears. And then the call of the noises in the shadows became too much for him. And, like a lighter streak in the darkness, he was gone.

She had been dreading the moment. But, watching him go, Christy realised that it was herself, as well as Mauw, that she was releasing; that she would have been no happier than the cat in the restricted domestic setting she had been trying to create. Sam had seen her faithfully through one phase of her life, and for that, she had loved him. But now he was dead, and it was time for her to move on.

Whatever happened, her life when she returned to England would be very different from what it had been before. And she felt a sudden sympathy for her father. She would never be happy, living his gypsy existence—but she suddenly saw that perhaps he too, like Mauw, had needed his freedom. People—and cats—didn't change. But you loved them anyway. . .

But her moment of insight was rudely shattered by the sound of footsteps crunching on the gravel and Brand's voice; harsh, preoccupied.

'What the hell are you doing round there? I heard the car pull up about ten minutes ago. Now for God's sake come and tell me what I'm doing wrong—I can't get a bloody thing out of this computer of yours.'

He turned abruptly and strode back to the house. Leaving the basketwork cage where it lay in the shadows, Christy picked up her overnight bag and stumbled after him.

The magic was shattered, the dress nothing but an ungainly hobble around her knees as she hurried to keep up. Tears stung her eyes, but she blinked them back, smothering them with a resolute layer of professionalism.

Emotions could come later. Right now she needed to think. She followed Brand's lowering figure through the elegant hallway and into the large room where she had installed the computer terminal the day before.

Then, it had been just that—a large, empty room. Now it could only be described as a ballroom. Light glittered on period furniture from two massive crystal chandeliers but, for all the grandeur, the only thing she had eyes for was the polished walnut table on a dais at one side of the room. On which, looking decidedly out of place in its modernity, stood the computer.

'Whatever I ask for, it bleeps and says "No data",' Brand said savagely. 'For God's sake, do something. People will be arriving in less than an hour.'

Sitting down in front of the blank screen, Christy's mind spun with possibilities. *What could be wrong?* She had tested the system exhaustively when installing the terminal, so why should it go wrong now? Experience told her that it was most likely something quite simple. . .

Brand was new to the computer, after all; probably he had just forgotten the correct way to operate the system.

'Right,' she said calmly, her voice devoid of emotion. 'Now I want you to show me exactly what you did. . .'

* * *

But five minutes later, Christy was anything but calm. 'I don't understand it,' she muttered, feverishly typing instruction after instruction in a vain hope that something—anything—would have escaped the mysterious blight that seemed to have hit the computer. 'All that data. . . I saw it, Brand—it was there—I checked it over and over. A whole week's work. . . And now there's nothing there. It just isn't possible. . .'

'It's possible, Christy. It's happened.' Now that he knew the worst, Brand's anger seemed to have frozen to an icy coolness. 'So what are you going to do about it? Is the system completely wrecked?'

'Well, no. . .' She ran her hand distractedly through her carefully blow-dried hair, oblivious now to everything except the problem that faced them. 'The system's fine—it's just lost its memory, if you like. All that information about your company the girls have been feeding in, all those figures—they've been wiped out. I just don't see how——'

'Forget about how it happened. That's history.' Behind the calm, she could hear a growing desperation in his voice. 'Can you fix it, that's the important question. And can you do it in——' he glanced at his watch '—in fifty-nine minutes?'

Less than an hour! 'I don't know, Brand,' she said helplessly. At the back of her mind, was the feeling that she was missing something; something she should have known all along. If only there was time to think things through. There was something that just wasn't right. . .

'There's a copy.' She wrenched her mind back to

the immediate problem. 'I took an extra copy when
the girls finished and put it in the safe. But it would
probably take an hour or more to re-load—and I'd
have to go across to the office to do it. That's going
to take another half-hour, even at this time of night.'

'That's too long. The guests will be arriving at nine.
Unless. . .'

An idea seemed suddenly to strike him, and he
dived across the room to where a telephone was
discreetly concealed against the panelling. 'If we can
catch Rainbow—you said she was working late these
days. She may not have left yet. Could you give her
instructions over the phone? That way we might
have a chance.'

'I suppose so.' Christy watched as he dialled the
number, conscious of an odd sense of premonition,
of danger. . . Like a thousand alarm bells ringing
somewhere a long way away. 'Brand, I don't
think——'

'Rainbow! Thank goodness you're there.' Brand's
face was animated now as he reeled off his instructions, one finger stabbing the air as if to emphasise
the urgency. Christy found herself watching that
finger as if hypnotised; watching it stabbing, stabbing. Like Rainbow's slim fingers on the computer
keys. . .

'Now listen, we've got a problem with the computer, but there's a copy of the data in the safe and
Christy's going to talk you through a re-load. Do you
think you can do that? Good girl. The safe combination is——'

'No!' As the pieces of her mental jigsaw finally

slotted together, Christy flung herself on to the phone, knocking the receiver out of Brand's grasp and sending it crashing against the wall.

'It's her,' she blurted incoherently as he looked at her in amazement. 'She did it! That's why she was reading the manuals. . . You said it wasn't like Rainbow to work late so often. I knew it wasn't possible for something like this to happen by accident. Don't you see, it was deliberate sabotage!'

Brand looked at her sceptically, picking up the receiver and covering the mouthpiece with his hand. 'Don't you think you're overreacting Christy? Rainbow's been with Sutcliffe's ever since she left school. Surely it's more likely that the computer just malfunctioned?'

She shook her head, searching for the words that would convince him. Could he really be so blind to Rainbow's jealousy? But if to him it had been just a casual liaison. . . But Christy found she couldn't bear to betray the other girl's feelings.

'I know it must seem like that to you, but computers are my business,' she said desperately, concentrating on the logical arguments. 'You get to know what sort of things happen by accident and this is too tidy. I knew at once that it didn't ring true, though I didn't put two and two together until now. Someone did this deliberately. And that's my professional opinion.'

He still didn't believe her; she could see it in his face. She tried again. 'Brand, at the moment your only copy of that information is locked in that safe. If I'm right, and if you give Rainbow the combination,

I wouldn't mind betting that there will be some kind of "problem" on the re-load. It wouldn't be difficult to arrange. Even if you don't believe me, is it really worth the risk of losing a whole week's preparation?'

'I'm not sure I have the choice.' Slowly he raised the phone to his ear, his hand still blocking off the sound. 'That computer has to be seen to be working by nine forty-three, or I'm out of business, Christy. As I see it, Rainbow's our only hope.

Seen to be working. . . 'She might not be,' Christy said slowly. 'Brand, I've got an idea. If you could tell me what kind of questions people are likely to ask, I could mock something up—just program the answers in. I've done it often enough when I've had to produce a demo at short notice.'

She watched in agony as the emotions flashed across Brand's face. Then at last he took his hand away and spoke into the phone. 'Rainbow? Sorry; forget about the re-load. We've decided it isn't practical tonight.' There was obviously some protest from the other end, because Christy saw his eyes suddenly narrow.

'I said forget it, Rainbow. And I think you've worked late enough tonight—you don't want to miss the reception. I'll call security and let them know you're leaving now.' He put the phone down sharply and Christy felt her heart soar in relief. He was halfway to believing her. Now all they had to do was make her idea work.

'Brand, you're sure you can arrange for someone to ask the right questions?'

Now that they were committed to her plan, Christy felt a sudden lack of confidence. Outside in the hallway, she could hear cymbals clashing discordantly as the troupe of Chinese musicians prepared their instruments. Brand had explained to her that they would perform the celebratory Lion Dance to bring good luck to the reborn company. And the guests would be here any minute. . .

'Remember, the computer doesn't know anything except those five answers,' she added anxiously. 'If that's not enough——'

'Don't worry, little rabbit. No one's really interested in the computer.'

In contrast to her own nervousness, Brand seemed to have recovered his good humour completely. No one could have guessed that his whole future hung on this demonstration, she thought with a pang.

'Once they've seen it answer a couple of queries, that'll be it.' He grinned, and she suddenly realised that he was enjoying himself. Enjoying the danger. . .

'And if it isn't?'

If she had hoped to provoke a reaction, she was disappointed. Brand just shrugged. 'In that case, I'll distract their attention—so be ready to back me up. I've got an idea or two up my sleeve.' It sounded intriguing, but before she could ask what he meant his face had suddenly changed.

'What's in the bag, Christy?' He was looking at her little case as though seeing it for the first time and his words were as careful as footsteps on thin ice.

'My night-things.' It was as though all the noise

around them fell silent. Waiting. . . 'I'd—I'd like to stay, Brand. If I may.'

The silence deepened, so that for one moment she thought he was angry. But then he reached out a hand and gently ruffled her hair. 'You know, they're almost completely hidden tonight.'

'What are?' Christy put her own hand to her hair in puzzlement. There was nothing there.

'Your ears, of course.' Brand grinned at her with a smile that turned her legs to water. 'Your soft, grey, timid, baby-rabbit ears.'

He pulled her towards him and she followed willingly, linking her arms around his waist and burying her face in his shirt. The wholesome, freshly laundered smell of the linen seemed to mingle with the scent of his body into something far more potent. Something as intoxicating as wine. . .

'By the way, I don't think I mentioned when you came in that you look absolutely stunning in that dress. Very remiss of me, but I had other things on my mind. So can I say it now?'

Christy felt herself light up in the warmth of his admiration. 'If you like,' she teased.

'You look absolutely stunning in that dress.'

But despite her happiness, the voice of caution inside her refused to be stilled. 'It's so risky, Brand. You could lose everything. . .

He sighed with mock despair and pulled her closer. 'Come here, Christy.' She could hear his voice rumbling through his chest. 'Don't tell me you don't get a kick out of the thought of fooling a whole roomful of Hong Kong's most influential windbags into believing that box of yours holds the secrets of the universe—when all it really knows is what we've pumped into it in the last twenty minutes? Where's your sense of adventure? I know you've got one— I've seen you eat bamboo-fungus soup, remember?'

Her face wrinkled at the memory. 'I suppose I have.' She nuzzled deeper into his chest, feeling a touch of his own recklessness affect her. It *was* rather funny. All those people. . .

She started to laugh and he bent towards her, gently tilting her face to look him in the eyes. His breath was warm on her lips. 'Welcome to the human race, Christy,' he murmured. 'I think you're ready to move on. To the last lesson.'

His lips touched hers, lightly, questioningly. Asking a question that sent a tremble of anticipation coursing through her flesh.

'Yes, teacher,' she whispered. And abandoned herself to the kiss.

'Meet Charlie Duncan. Charlie, this is Christy Maynard, whose company produces this box of tricks.'

Christy looked up to see a bluff, jolly-looking man with a short white beard and a definite Naval air about him. 'How do you do?' she said politely, feeling her way. 'Are you one of Brand's business colleagues?'

Both men laughed. 'Old Charlie hasn't done a stroke of work since he escaped from the Navy,' Brand explained with an affection for the older man that was unmistakable. 'He just hangs about the yacht club, making a nuisance of himself—or so I've heard. They don't let me in there, of course.'

He grinned, as if at some private joke. 'Anyway, look after him, will you? There's a couple of people I want to talk to before I start things rolling. And keep him away from the rum. There's only ten minutes to go before the deadline.'

Brand moved swiftly away into the thickening crowd of people towards two men in grey suits who stood by the wall close to the door. The party atmosphere that swirled around them seemed to leave the men untouched, and the fanciful notion occurred to Christy that the greyness would go right through. . .

The thought made her shiver, and she turned back to her companion. 'Why did he say that, Mr Duncan? About the yacht club not letting him in?'

The old man shook his head. 'Call me Charlie, my dear. And it's true enough in a way; years ago when he applied to join, his brother Jocelyn was a member and blocked the application. No love lost between those two.'

'I hated his guts'. . . Christy remembered the bitterness she had heard in his voice and shivered. 'Oh, I see. But surely now. . .?'

'Oh, now they'd take him like a shot. Jocelyn was never popular, but of course he had influence. Only now, you couldn't drag Brand within ten yards of the place. He keeps that tub of his tied up in some God-awful typhoon shelter with the junks; says the company's more select. Don't know how he doesn't get murdered in his bunk.'

He paused absent-mindedly to knock back half of his drink. 'But then he's always been thick with that lot—spent more time speaking Chinese than he did English, as a kid. Jocelyn gave him a hard time. . . Couldn't really blame him for hitting back.' The old man seemed almost to have forgotten she was there, engrossed in his stream of reminiscence. 'But a woman, though. . .'

He started, as if suddenly waking from a dream. 'Excuse me, m'dear. Rambling on. Old story, best forgotten really. But young Brand never did know how to bury his hatchets.'

Christy had the curious feeling that there was another story mixed in with his ramblings; a story she didn't understand. . . But just then, there was a clash of cymbals and Brand's voice cut through the babble of noise in the room.

'Ladies and gentlemen! The auspicious moment approaches! This is a big day for Sutcliffe's; the day when we step out of the eighteenth century and into the twenty-first. So if you'll stand back and let my resident expert through. . .'

Christy felt her mouth dry with fear as she made her way through the crowd, feeling the curious eyes plucking at her, probing her. But there was excitement there too. And as she sat down at the computer she felt, for the first time in her life, a flicker of understanding for what motivated men like her father. Men like Brand. . .

Except that Brand was like no man she had ever

known. He stood by her shoulder as the drum rolled, towering over her like a rock. There was a clash of cymbals, and then the sound died away, leaving the room caught in an expectant web of silence.

She flicked on the switch and entered the password. The screen before her flickered into life. Her fingertips on the keyboard were damp and slippery with tension. There was a sudden clamour of enquiry from the crowd. And then, miraculously, from behind her she heard a female voice. Asking the first of their prepared questions.

It had to be a female, of course. Christy felt a pang of ridiculous jealousy, even though in the same moment she recognised that it had been clever of Brand to give his question to a woman. That way, it seemed like natural courtesy for him to pick it out of the babble. But she found herself wishing she could see what the questioner looked like.

The next two enquiries came pat. And then something went wrong. Nowhere in the barrage of questions was one she recognised. . . She could feel Brand's tension beside her like a tightened spring. Mounting. . .

And then he had switched off the computer and taken her hand, and was pulling her to the centre of the dais. Christy followed, bewildered. And watched him hold up his hand for silence.

'My friends. . . The *Fung Shui* master has assured me that today is the best day in a hundred years for beginning new ventures. And I have to admit to a deception. I have asked you here tonight to witness, not one new beginning, but two. Because when I went to England to find the computer system you have just seen, I found something more. Something beautiful. . .'

He spun Christy round to face him and a murmur of anticipation rippled through the audience. But Christy only felt numb. It couldn't be that. . . He couldn't be so cruel. . .

'I found Christy.' As if hurtling towards an accident, she could see what was coming. And she was powerless to stop it.

'And I want her to be my wife.'

CHAPTER EIGHT

THE drums rolled and cymbals crashed, and the great red and gold Lion leapt into frenzied action. But Christy was hardly aware of the uproar in the room.

Trapped inside her own private bubble of suffering, she watched herself go through the motions that were expected of her—that Brand expected of her. 'I've got something up my sleeve—just be ready to back me up. . .' At that moment, she hated him. And yet he couldn't know the anguish his showmanship had caused.

Nor could she deny that, as an audience distraction, his flamboyant proposal had been an unqualified success, generating more excitement and good will than the rest of the opening ceremony put together. As the Lion weaved through the guests, prancing and leaping and fluttering its giant eyelashes, the atmosphere in the ballroom was more like a successful political meeting than a business reception. . . Staring fixedly at Brand's shirt-front, Christy did her best to mime delighted acceptance through a veil of tears.

'Look at me, Christy.' His voice was no more than a whisper, but there was a note in it that cut through the babble of noise and congratulation that surrounded them. It spoke to her directly; intimate as a caress and as unignorable as the blade of a knife.

Reluctantly she raised her eyes to his, to see in them an unmistakable blaze of triumph. . . And something more. Something that made her heart pound with unspeakable hope.

'Brand. . .' she whispered. 'Brand, are you sure?'

'Of course.' He bent down to plant a kiss on her upturned forehead, but as he drew back, something caught his eye.

'I have to disappear for a while now, Christy,' he murmured. 'I have to talk business with—my friends.' Glancing down from the low platform, Christy could see the impassive faces of the men she had noticed earlier, waiting like grey rocks as the party swirled round them. 'Wait for me.'

'I'll wait.' She watched him drop lithely down into the throng and melt through it with as little effort as a swimmer, carving through water. And at that moment, she felt she would wait forever.

Only, with his going, Christy found she was thrown defenceless to the wolves. He had left her the centre of attention, and there was nowhere to escape. Unable to help herself, she was tossed from group to group like a rag doll at a children's party. And ended up nearly as frayed.

There seemed to be no end to it, no time to stand back and think. Cameras flashed in her face as the newsmen who had turned up for the opening fell like sharks on this plum addition to their story. And the questions and congratulations which buffeted her ranged from the apparently sincere to the pointedly bitchy.

'No, I didn't know he was going to. . .' She knew

nothing; nothing. For a moment, she felt a new panic closing in. What if, to him, this was no more than a game. . .? But the memory of what she had seen in his eyes sustained her.

'Yes, it was a surprise.' Somehow, she forced a smile. 'No, I have no idea; we haven't talked about children. . .' She felt the smile stretch thinner and thinner over her face, as if it would crack with tension. 'I expect it was just an impulse; he's an impulsive sort of man. . .'

'He certainly is.'

It was Rainbow's voice. Christy spun round and for a second the Chinese girl let her mask drop. The naked hostility that she saw there made Christy shiver with fear. As if in the presence of a snake.

'You are a brave woman, Miss Maynard.' The mask was back in place; the lisping voice sickly sweet over the poisoned words. But the challenge was unmistakable.

The group that clustered around them fell unnaturally silent, and Christy could feel their eyes on her, waiting. 'A very brave woman,' Rainbow went on. 'To take such a. . .*dangerous* husband.'

'I don't know what you mean, Rainbow.' Christy struggled to keep her voice light and turned, meaning to move casually away. But the Chinese girl's next words stopped her in mid-movement.

'You must be very certain of your power, Miss Maynard. Or the rewards must be very great. After all, when a man has killed one of his women, it must take a certain—determination, shall we say?—to be the next in line.'

A shocked hiss ran round the company, and Christy could feel the silence spreading to adjacent groups. As if the wolves had scented blood.

'Unless you didn't know. . .?' Rainbow's voice was delicately probing and sharp as a surgeon's knife. And suddenly nothing mattered more than wiping the cruel smile from her face.

'Oh, I can assure you that I know exactly what kind of man I am marrying, Rainbow dear. But then so do you—now.'

She turned to the woman next to her with a brittle laugh. 'Rainbow here has been trying a little petty sabotage in her spare time.' The girl's face hardly flickered, but there was a rigidity to her smile that told Christy the shot had hit home. 'So amusing. . . Of course, Mr Sutcliffe spotted it at once. And now, if you will excuse me, I really must be moving on——'

But as she turned blindly away, Christy bumped into the familiar figure of Charlie Duncan, pushing his way through the crush towards her. Her face must have shown her relief.

'Come on, m'dear,' he said grimly, linking his arm in hers. 'I'm taking you out of this. Sutcliffe had no damned business leaving you to face that pack of hyenas on your own.'

He steered her firmly out of the doorway and across the hall into a dark panelled room that seemed to be a cross between study and library, calling to one of the waiters as he did so. Not until she was settled deep into a soft leather armchair with a balloon glass of brandy pressed into her now openly trembling hands did he encourage her to speak.

'So what the hell was that unpleasant little cat saying to you?' he said at last. 'I've never seen a woman go as white as you did without actually falling down. And don't tell me it was nothing. You're not the sort of girl to be knocked back by a bitchy remark.'

Christy took a sip of the spirit and felt the smooth fire spread its warmth through her veins. 'You don't even know me,' she said unsteadily, playing for time. 'How do you know what I'm like?' Despite his kindness, she felt a strange reluctance to confide in the old man, as if by telling him she might confirm her fears. As if she was afraid of what he might be able to tell her.

'You don't get to my age without picking up a few tips about human nature.' He looked at her appraisingly. 'You've got character—and courage. And if you're planning on marrying Brand Sutcliffe you'll need both.'

'That's what she said. . .' Charlie's unwitting echo of her tormentor's words forced the response from her throat. And once she had started, it seemed easier to continue. 'Charlie, she said Brand had killed one of his women. . . What did she mean? Everyone else seemed to know. She said Brand was *dangerous*.'

'So that was it. And I suppose Sutcliffe hadn't warned you. . .?' Christy shook her head and her companion took a sip of his own drink as if to foritify himself. 'No, I guessed as much. He's a fool—it was bound to come out. Look, I'm not sure I shouldn't leave this to Brand——'

'No!' Christy's hand clenched so tightly round the stem of her balloon glass that she felt the base cut into her palm. 'Please, you have to tell me what all this is about. I can't go back in there till I know—and even when Brand gets back, he won't be free to talk until the reception is over.'

The old man still looked doubtful, and she added fiercely, 'I seem to be the only one in the room still in ignorance—if you don't enlighten me, I'm sure someone else will. And surely I have a right to know? He's asked me to marry him, for God's sake. I'm entitled to know the truth.'

'Yes. Yes, you are.' Charlie looked at her compassionately. 'Only when you've lived in Hong Kong as long as I have, m'dear, you'll realise that truth can be an elusive quality. I can't tell you the truth about this; only Sutcliffe can do that. But I'll tell you what I know.'

He stopped, and seemed to be casting about for a place to start, then, just as Christy was about to prompt him again, said abruptly, 'How much has Brand told you about his brother?'

'Jocelyn? Only that they—didn't get on.' But the euphemistic phrase seemed weak beside the memory of Brand's bitterness. She expanded grimly. 'Brand said he hated his guts. I know that Jocelyn won control of Sutcliffe's in a bet on a sailing race. And that Brand went away and didn't come back until his brother was killed.'

'So you didn't know about Melissa?'

'No.' She squeezed the word out through a throat numb with apprehension. 'Is she. . .?'

'She was Brand's fiancée. Totally unsuited, in my opinion, but he was a lot younger then. And there was no denying she was beautiful enough to warp any man's judgement. But I always thought she was a hard bitch, and as it turned out I was right.'

Charlie paused and took another sip of his drink. 'Damn the man, he should have told you this. When Brand lost Sutcliffe's to his brother, he didn't see Melissa for dust. Two months later she was married to Joss. It looked like she'd been keeping her options open all along. I think that's what decided Brand to clear out altogether.'

'I see. But why——? I thought Jocelyn's wife died with him in a helicopter accident.'

'She did.' The old man looked down, avoiding Christy's eyes. 'He should have told you this,' he said again. 'The talk was that the crash wasn't accidental.' His words seemed to drop like stones into the silence. 'The talk was that Brand had arranged it.'

For a moment, Christy just stared at him in horror. And when she spoke, she hardly recognised her voice as her own. 'But that's rubbish, surely?' she whispered. 'Brand wouldn't. . .' But even as she spoke she could hear her own lack of conviction. She knew so little about him. Who was she to predict what Brand Sutcliffe would or wouldn't do? Only his fiancée. . . His second fiancée. And the first one had died.

She reached out to the old man, begging for

reassurance. 'Charlie, it's not true, is it? It's just a rumour. . .'

Charlie looked at her and opened his mouth to reply. But the bluff reassurance she had hoped for didn't come. 'I don't know,' he said at last. 'I'm sorry, m'dear, but you don't want pretty lies. I don't think he did it; the Brand Sutcliffe I know and like wouldn't have done it. But he never denied it, and that looked black against him. And there's a part of him I've never really known.'

'What do you mean?' But she knew what he meant. Hadn't she felt it, that darkness behind his eyes? That feeling of *danger*?

Charlie shifted uncomfortably in his seat. 'Look, don't take me wrong, m'dear. I don't think he did it—and I do know he was in Australia when it happened, so there was no question of a direct involvement. But he has some dangerous friends. That crowd in the junks—the Chinese have a different attitude to life and death from ours. And Brand was practically brought up by them.'

He snorted and shook his head. 'Blame his father myself,' he went on. 'Fool couldn't see the boy for Joss; but that's by the way. The point is that if it wasn't an accident—and there seems to have been some evidence that it wasn't—then Brand was the only person to benefit. And by a considerable amount.'

'No. . .' But it was a whisper of pain, not of denial.

The old man looked suddenly very tired. 'I told you, I don't—I can't—really believe he was responsible. Maybe some of his friends decided to do him a favour. . . But there's only one person who knows the truth. And it's him you should be asking.' He stood up, and reached out a hand. 'Come on, m'dear. It's time to go back. You've got courage; don't let them get you down.'

But as she followed him back to the party, her head held high, Christy knew she had never felt less courageous in her life.

She felt Brand, rather than saw him, the moment he re-entered the room almost an hour later. The instant awareness of his presence sent prickles of apprehension down her spine. Turning away from the local dignitary who was monopolising her attention, Christy watched as Brand made his way towards her through the crowd.

'Well done, little rabbit. We did it.' He ruffled her hair teasingly, his face alight with the intoxication of success, his own exalted mood blinding him to the coolness of her own response.

'They've signed the agreement, then?' It was hardly necessary to ask, but she had to say something, had to break the silence that squeezed her throat like a clenched fist.

Christy stared up at the man who had—so publicly, so flamboyantly—asked her to marry him. The man who had swept her from the stability she had painstakingly built for herself and set her adrift in a sea of emotions that threatened at every wave to overtake her. And as she looked, she felt inside her the dull ache of recognition.

She had seen that look of triumph before, that air

of heightened excitement that shone from him like flame from a victory beacon. That fierce gambler's joy. On her father's face she had seen it many times. And she had seen its shadow too; the dark depression that tore at her heart when, inevitably, things went wrong and he was left staring at the broken shards of his latest dream.

Brand was still talking, sweeping her off for a triumphal progress round the room. His presence seemed to electrify everyone with whom he came in contact, making the party hum with life. But Christy felt nothing. Only a cold stone of certainty that seemed to have replaced her heart.

With ruthless savagery, he had won back the company from his brother—and taken revenge on the woman who had stolen his heart. Christy seemed to see his face waver and change before her eyes. And behind the man—triumphant and laughing and dear—she saw the cruel face of the pirate. . .

The bitterness of his betrayal ate deep into her bones. Now, using her as a weapon, the pirate had won this battle, too. His star was in the ascendancy; his *joss* was good. But one day, the tables would be turned on Brand Sutcliffe and the shadow would engulf him.

And when it was, she wouldn't be there to weep for him.

It wouldn't be she who shared his gambler's pain.

'So what's the matter, Christy?'

Now that they were finally alone, Christy felt her resolution fail. It was late, and her legs trembled with weariness. Tomorrow. . .she would ask him tomorrow.

'Nothing.' She tried to smile, but it didn't quite work. 'Honestly, Brand. I'm—I'm just so tired. If your chauffeur could drop me back at the hotel——'

'At the hotel?' Brand raised an eyebrow. 'So that's it; the rabbit is on the run again.' His voice had a husky edge of desire that stirred an answering tremor deep inside her. 'There's no need for you to go back tonight, Christy. We are engaged, after all.' He smiled as he said it, his mouth twisting in a sensuous curve, teasing her. 'Besides, I had the impression you were planning to stay even when we weren't. . .'

Christy had to fight the urge to give up; to allow her head to rest forward on to his chest and let his warmth thaw the chill within her. To snatch at what shreds of happiness she could, before the inevitable happened and the differences between them tore them apart. But his next words gave her strength.

'I thought that was a brilliant touch of mine, the engagement.' His smile was open now, half laughing, remembering his own cleverness. 'It really did the trick. And you played up perfectly—I must admit there was a second when I wondered if you would.'

Christy remembered that second, when pain had lanced through her like a knife. She had seen the truth, then. Before he had blinded her with that look of hunger in his eyes and made her believe that perhaps, somehow, their lives might touch. That he might want them to. . .

More fool her. Because it had been nothing but a calculated move in his game. Christy felt the renewed pain that twisted inside her with that knowledge give her the strength of anger. Her tiredness and fear forgotten, she turned on him, fiercely.

'Well, I hope the contracts are signed and sealed,' she almost spat. 'Because I have no intention of playing the part of loving fiancée for another second.'

She had the satisfaction of seeing shock-waves momentarily distort that damnably heart-rendingly handsome face. So it *was* still important to him to preserve the fiction. Perhaps the deal wasn't finalised. . . Christy felt a bitter pleasure in the thought that she might still have the power to destroy what he had paid for with her agony.

'I'm flying back to England on the next free flight,' she flung at him. 'And there's nothing you can do to stop me. If you were counting on a long, face-saving engagement before you dump me, you'll be disappointed. So unless you intend to kill me too——'

She hadn't meant to say that. Oh, God, she hadn't meant to say that. His hand jerked up, and Christy flinched away, feeling a surge of real terror as she realised where her angry tongue had led her.

But the expected blow never landed, although she saw the veins on his forearm stand out like cords as his fist clenched in fury. The silence seemed to go on for ever. And when at last he spoke, the rasping control in his voice was more chilling than any anger.

'Who have you been talking to? Who told you about Melissa?'

So he wasn't even going to try and pretend ignorance. Until that moment, Christy hadn't realised just how desperately some part of her had been praying to hear Brand deny the terrible story. When he didn't, it was like a kind of death. But it gave her a reckless courage. When you were dead, there was nothing that could hurt you any more. . .

'Half the territory, if you must know,' she said waspishly. 'Did you really think you could keep it quiet? Multiple murder is hardly the sort of incident that's likely to slip people's minds—even in Hong Kong.'

'Damn, I should never have left you alone.' Brand's fist flew out to strike one of the smooth white columns in a futile gesture of frustration. 'If I'd been there, they'd never have dared——'

Christy listened to his ranting with a strange feeling of calm. All he cared about was that his plans had been thwarted. . . Even now, there was no word of regret for the pain she had suffered; no claim of innocence, however empty, of the crime with whch he'd been charged. It was as if he had almost forgotten her presence.

And then he looked at her. She flinched back in fear, and his face changed.

'I see,' he said softly. The menace in his voice made her shiver. 'So I'm tried, convicted and hung already, am I? Without a word to say in my defence?' He paused, as if waiting for Christy to speak. But she was paralysed; like a rabbit cowering under the gaze of a snake.

'In that case, there is only one thing I can do.' His eyes never left her as he stepped back towards the door and thrust it open. It slammed back against the hinges, the noise echoing like a gunshot through the silent house. 'Chan Lu!'

Almost immediately, the little chauffeur was at Brand's shoulder, his lack of inches only emphasising his master's height and towering strength. Together, they seemed to fill the room with threat. Christy's legs were shaking, and a swirling blackness seemed to fill her brain. But she fought back the weakness. Somewhere in her mind was the terrible thought that if she fainted now she might never wake up.

'Bring the car round, Chan Lu.' Brand's eyes were still fixed on her, as if they could scorch her with their heat. As if he hated her. 'Miss Maynard and I are going on a little trip.'

Obediently, the man melted away, his face impassive. Christy looked desperately behind her for a way of escape, but there was none. At last she found her voice.

'You can't do this,' she whispered.

'Oh, but I can, I promise you. I can do just exactly as I like. And don't look to Chan Lu for help. He's absolutely loyal. I could kill you now and ask him to dispose of the body and he wouldn't turn a hair.'

Christy believed him. Brand's anger had transformed him, finally and completely, into the stranger she had always known lurked threateningly behind those eyes. She looked up at him soundlessly, not even daring to plead.

He spoke again, and the smile that twisted his mouth was animal, like a snarl. 'He would obey me without question, Christy—and you would be well advised to do the same. Now, we're going for a drive. And be sensible. If you scream, no one will hear you. But it might oblige me to shut you up.'

Afterwards, she never knew how she managed to get through that nightmare journey without breaking. But somehow, despite her terror, there was a core of disbelief to her fear, as if she knew she was dreaming and would eventually wake up. As if a part of her couldn't forget Brand's words in the pirate cave. . .

'Trust me. . .' She could almost hear his voice speaking to her in the darkness. And, ridiculous as it was, she felt comforted.

Outside the tinted windows of the car, the blackness of the Peak gave way to city lights, then darkened again as they drove on into the night. It might have been minutes or hours before the Rolls-Royce pulled smoothly to a halt. Time seemed to have been temporarily suspended, the ticking of clocks replaced by the still thunderous beating of her own heart. She heard the door unlock automatically beside her.

'Out.'

As Christy stepped obediently from the car's cushioned interior, the tang of salt in the air and the gentle slap-slapping of water nearby told her at once that they were at the waterfront. A vision of her body bobbing in the oily waters of the harbour rose up in front of her, and the panic surged again, quickening her pulse as if for flight.

But a steadier instinct told her that there was no point trying to run. And as if to confirm her thoughts,

Brand's hand came down to grip her arm. His fingers bit cruelly into her flesh.

'Down here.'

Her eyes were still unaccustomed to the darkness and she stumbled as he pushed her forwards down a rickety wooden ramp which bobbed and swayed with their weight. Brand stopped, and she heard him whistle through his fingers; once, twice, three times. Was it an echo, or was there an answering whistle? Christy strained her ears and eyes into the darkness. Where were they? And what did her captor plan to do?

The silence stretched from seconds into minutes, her nerves stretching with it almost to breaking-point. And then, suddenly, the ramp they were standing on lurched, almost throwing her off her balance, and she realised with a start that they were walking along a ramshackle jetty only a few feet above the water.

It was the clue her mind needed to start making sense of their surroundings. No wonder she had smelt the sea. The towering shapes that rose above them were not buildings but boats—junks. She was in the middle of a floating city, surrounded by thousands of people. But they were his people, not hers, and the thought made her feel even more alone.

Until there was a sound behind her, and the jetty lurched again. And Christy realised that the new arrival was not some sinister-looking junk-dweller come to help her employer dispose of his now inconvenient fiancée, but a cheerfully tousled

Chinese boy of about fourteen with a gap-toothed smile and an air of having just woken up.

'Hi, Mista Brand. You want we go out tonight?' A frown creased his skinny face. 'Radio not fixed yet, Mista Brand. And weather——' He stopped in mid-sentence, seeming to take in Christy's presence for the first time, and his grin broadened knowingly. 'Sorry, Mista Brand. You no going sailing, I think. You just want I clear off, yes?'

'Got it in one.' Brand's voice was light, but Christy could still feel his fingers gripping her arm and knew that the steel was still there. 'You can go and pester that long-suffering sister of yours for a change.'

'Right on, skipper.' The boy scuttled off back up the jetty without a backward glance. From his casual acceptance, it wasn't exactly unusual for Brand to throw him out whenever he wanted a night of privacy with his current lady. Christy was startled by the clear thrust of jealousy that pierced through her at the thought. Had he brought Melissa here? Or Rainbow?

But as the vibration of the boat-boy's steps died away Brand was forcing her down some slippery steps into a small dinghy that, even with the dark to hide the worst of its faults, looked dangerously unseaworthy to her eyes. And Christy felt the fear press in on her again, driving out those other disturbing emotions.

She tried to pull back, but heard a movement behind her. The menacing figure of Brand's chauffeur was still on watch in the shadow of the harbour wall.

That made her decide. Instinctively, she knew that

if she had a chance it was with Brand alone—not
with his frighteningly impassive henchman. Alone,
she might be able to appeal to the other Brand
Sutcliffe, if he still existed—if he had ever existed. If
the whisper inside her head which still insisted he
did was anything but a delusion. . .

She had to believe he did. It was madness—but
there was no other choice left open to her. Abandon-
ing her attempts at resistance, Christy stepped gingerly into the boat. There was a faint splash as Brand
pushed their little craft off from the jetty. And then
nothing but the almost silent movement of the blades
through the water, as they slipped away into the
winding passageways that made up the water-borne
city.

Christy watched his hands on the oars, the muscles
twisting with economical effort as he propelled them
forwards. His face was shrouded in darkness. But
there was something obscurely comforting about his
hands.

So this was *Moondancer*. Christy hardly had time to
take in the pale gleam of the scrubbed wooden decks
and the ghostly shapes of masts and tight-rolled sails
before she was pushed unceremoniously towards the
low, black doorway in the centre of the cockpit.

'Get down below.' His voice had regained a new
edge of anger, as if the contact between their bodies
had re-fuelled a fire. 'I don't want to see you till
we're somewhere we can talk in private.' Reaching
into the void, he switched on a dim glow of light.

'And don't get any fantasies about calling the coast-guard—the radio's out of order. The bunk in the saloon is made up; you might as well get some sleep.'

He followed her down, and she was vaguely aware of him flicking switches and fiddling with what she presumed was the radio. But if it was, his diagnosis had been correct. Nothing issued from it except some high-pitched squeals and she heard him swear under his breath.

Then he climbed back up into the darkness and left her alone. Christy looked around her. Two narrow bench seats were built into the wood-panelled sides of the cabin, and one was made up as a bed with threadbare sheets and a pillow that smelled of damp.

Above her, she could hear the roar of an engine starting up, followed by a steady throb. A heartbeat.

At the back of her mind was a nagging feeling that she was missing something, that there was something she should have known. And she associated it for some reason with those broad, strong muscled hands. . .

But her mind was spinning away in disconnected circles of its own, owing nothing to logic. And as if this was any pleasure trip, as if she was not being hijacked into the middle of the ocean by a self-confessed murderer with every reason to see her as his next victim, as if there was nothing else in the world that mattered more, she fell on to the bunk and went to sleep.

CHAPTER NINE

SOMEONE was shaking her; shaking her awake. Only it wasn't just she who was shaking; the whole world seemed to be tossing and turning, as if a baby giant had suddenly decided to use it for a plaything.

'Christy.' The familiar deep voice was quietly insistent. 'Christy, wake up. You have to wake up and listen.'

'Brand? Where——?' But, as her eyes accustomed themselves to the muted lighting of the little cabin, Christy remembered where she was. Of course; she was on board *Moondancer*. Brand had brought her here. . . She felt a spasm of fear, but when she looked back at him there was no anger in his expression. Only a strange mixture of determination and—it looked like pity.

The boat lurched again, and Brand swore quietly under his breath. The oilskins he was now wearing were slick with water and his hair was plastered wet against his scalp. Under one arm he held a bundle of clothes.

'Look, Christy, I've got to go back up,' he said impatiently. 'But I need you to help me. Get up and get these things on and then come up. As quick as you can. Understand?'

'Yes, but. . .' As she sat up, the floor of the cabin seemed to drop suddenly away, the whole room

tilting violently on its axis. Christy felt her stomach
heave in sympathy. 'Brand, what's happening?'

'We've run into some rather lumpy weather, that's
all. Nothing *Moondancer* can't handle. But there's no
time to talk. I want to see you up top in two minutes
flat.'

Brand thrust the bundle of unpleasantly salt-stiff-
ened clothing into her arms, and, with the single
clipped word, 'Hurry,' turned and strode from the
room.

Despite the lurching of the ship beneath them, he
seemed to move as lightly as a cat, swaying with the
motion without apparent effort or thought. The full
significance of this didn't strike Christy until she
stood up and tried to emulate him—and found
herself thrown heavily and unceremoniously across
the cabin.

'Damn you, Brand Sutcliffe! You drag me out here
and then expect me to help sail your rotten boat. . .
What good do you think I'm going to be, if I can't
even stand up?'

But despite her rebellious mutterings, it didn't
occur to her to disobey Brand's instructions. There
had been something about his face that had brooked
no argument. Slowly and painfully, she struggled
out of her dress and into the clothes he had left her,
wrinkling her nose in disgust at their musty odour of
damp and salt.

It took far longer than two minutes. She was almost
completely dressed when she discovered that the
boots would have to be put on before the waterproof
trousers—and that meant stripping everything off

again to put it right. 'Just let him dare say anything,' she thought as she made a slow and precarious way along the passage and up the companionway ladder. 'Just let him dare. . .'

But as she poked her head up into the cockpit, Brand's only reaction was to thrust what looked like one end of a dog-lead at her.

'Good girl,' he said. 'Clip this to the loops in the front of your jacket.'

She obeyed him bemusedly. 'What is it?'

'A safety line. Look; I've clipped the other end to this strong point here.' He pointed to a metal ring sunk in the side of the cockpit. 'You'll find them dotted all over the ship.'

'But what's it for?'

'To stop you being swept overboard.' The laconic reply was like a slap in the face, and for the first time Christy started to realise that they might actually be in danger. . . But she didn't have time to consider it before he was hurrying her on.

'Get that hatch shut, or we'll be swimming down there when the next wave comes over.' Her movements were slow and clumsy in the bulky waterproofs and she could feel his impatience. 'Come on, Christy; we haven't got all day. I need you to take over the wheel while I get up there and reef down the sails.'

'What?' She was standing unsteadily in the cockpit now, exposed to the full fury of wind and spray, and she could feel the panic rising. 'I can't steer this boat, Brand.' How could he possibly expect her to do such a thing? 'I've never——'

'Then this is where you start.' His voice had a steely edge of determination in it. 'Listen to me, Christy. I don't have time to argue with you about every order I give. If I tell you to do something, you do it. Is that clear?'

She stared at him in furious silence. 'But I can't——'

'I said, *Is that clear?*'

She flinched as the words whipcracked through the noise of the wind. 'Yes, sir,' she said with angry emphasis. But he didn't seem to hear the sarcasm.

'Good. This wind is going to get worse before it gets better and I need to change the jib down and reef the main. But I don't want to lose more speed than I can help, so I want you to steer for me. You see that dial? That shows the boat's direction against the wind. Now I want you to steer so that the arrow stays at about ten o'clock.'

Christy found herself being pulled round so that she stood between his body and the wheel, her hands trapped beneath his on the smooth wooden surface. Despite the precariousness of their situation, she felt a tremor of excitement and hated him for the power he held over her.

'Then bring it round like this until it points to twelve o'clock. . .'

Above her, the sail started flapping madly, like a huge trapped bird. The noise was deafening. 'Brand!'

'Don't panic, little rabbit. That's what's supposed to happen. Now, take it back to ten o'clock and try it again. Feel how the sail tightens. . . That's it. Not too far. Now swing her back round until it flaps. . .'

His voice went on, calmly taking her through the movements he wanted her to make. And gradually Christy felt her panic subside. His body was pressed close against her in the confined space, as solid as the wood of the boat itself, and she could feel his strength flow through her like a physical force.

At last, he decided she was ready. 'So, keep it at ten until I raise my arm,' he repeated. 'Then round to twelve and hold it there until I raise my arm again. Don't over-correct, and take it slowly. Try to feel the boat. . . OK, little one?'

'I think so.' But when he slipped out from behind her, leaving her alone at the wheel, Christy felt some of her confidence evaporate. 'How long will it take us, Brand? To get back to port?'

For a moment, he stared at her uncomprehendingly. Then he laughed.

'We're not turning back, Christy. We're heading on—out to sea.' Before she could catch her breath to protest, he was making his way forward on the bucking deck towards the mast. And in the wind's rising fury she knew her pleas would go unheard.

By the time Brand raised his arm to signal that he had finished, Christy was drenched with sweat under her waterproofs and her arms trembled with tension. The little boat that had responded so obediently to Brand's control seemed to take on a life of its own under her hands, like a horse scenting an inexperienced rider.

More than once, she had turned the wheel the wrong way, causing the boat to tilt at a terrifying angle so that Brand, on the cabin roof, had to cling desperately to the mast for support.

She was cold and wet and scared. But most of all, she was angry, the fear she felt feeding the anger and swelling it to something like hatred for the man who had tossed her life into the air like tossing a coin for a bet.

Brand Sutcliffe had stolen her safety and drawn her into loving him. He had taken from her all the defences she had built up so painstakingly over the years. And he had given her nothing but danger in return.

Brand Sutcliffe was *dangerous*. She had known that from the start, but she had chosen to ignore it. And now she was paying the price.

When he finally climbed back down into the cockpit, the old sail bundled under one arm, Christy turned on him.

'You've got to turn back, Brand. We can't go on in this. You can't be serious——' But one look at his face convinced her that he was. She felt a flash of real, gut-wrenching fear. 'Brand, you're crazy! We can't possibly——'

'We've got no choice,' he interrupted curtly. 'If this is what I think it might be, we need as much searoom as we can get. We've got to put out to sea to ride it out. Or we'll be smashed to pieces on the rocks.'

His voice was grim, but there was a strange undercurrent of excitement that ran beneath the words. 'Now, I'll take the helm back while you get this sail bundled up and take it below. And make sure all the cupboards are shut and there's nothing lying loose to get thrown around. Then I'll get you tucked in for the duration. I want you safely out of the way by the time this thing really hits us.'

He was enjoying it, she realised, his pirate soul relishing the danger. But he was risking both their lives. . .

The hatred settled like a stone in Christy's stomach. Like an automaton, she moved hither and thither, obeying Brand Sutcliffe's orders as he steered the little ship further and further from land and safety. And all the time she hugged her anger to her, using it to drive away the fear.

'I'll try not to call you, but if I do, make sure you clip on to one of the strong-points before coming up into the cockpit.' Brand stood squarely in the centre of the cabin, a giant in Lilliput, his tall frame even bulkier in the heavy waterproofs. He pointed to the dog-lead that still hung from the front of her jacket. 'Don't take this off. Understand? Now I'll make sure you're strapped in.'

She watched numbly as he opened the bunk she had been sleeping on, took out a sleeping bag, and unrolled a great flap of canvas that ran almost the whole length of the bunk. Following his instructions, Christy lay down on the narrow bunk and wriggled fully clothed into the bag.

'What are you doing?' She twisted her head to see him tie the canvas to hooks on the ceiling above her head so it formed a rigid curtain, cutting her off from the rest of the cabin. The effect was claustrophobic, leaving only a small gap by her face. 'What is this, some kind of privacy arrangement? I hardly think. . . What if I want to get up?'

'I don't advise you to want to.' Brand's face was bleak as he looked down at her, but his voice was softer. 'It's not your privacy I'm worried about—it's your safety. The lee-cloth is there to stop you being thrown around the cabin if things get rough.' Digging into another locker, he pulled out a bucket and tied it to the bunk beside her head. 'And that's in case you get sick.

'Oh.' In her mind, Christy tried to visualise the sort of storm that could cause that amount of havoc. 'Brand, is this a typhoon?'

'I don't know, Christy. I hope to hell not. There was a storm reported a couple of days ago off the coast of China—we could be picking up the edge of that system. But I don't know how it's been developing; I've been incommunicado for the past two days, setting up that deal, and I haven't picked up the forecasts.' He shook his head. 'The barometer's dropping through the floor, which doesn't look good. I wish to God we had a radio.'

For a moment he looked vulnerable, humanly afraid. Christy had a fleeting vision of the tiny speck that would be *Moondancer* against the savage backcloth of the sea. And, smaller still, a man alone, fighting the elements. . . For a moment, she wanted to plead with him to hold her, to comfort her. To tell her that it was going to be all right.

But already she could tell his attention had left her. It was back with the boat, and the now wild flapping of the sails as *Moondancer* was left to manage without a helmsman. And then he was gone.

So instead, she remembered her anger. And wrapped herself in it to await the danger into which Brand Sutcliffe had so recklessly plunged her.

The noise was the worst thing; the awful, indescribable noise that filled her head and battered her senses. The crashes that made her expect every second that this was the blow that the little ship wouldn't survive; that this time the mast had snapped like a dry twig leaving them helpless; that this time the water would come pouring in to drown her in the confines of her bunk.

There would be a sickening moment of silence that was almost, but not quite, worse than the noise, and a feeling of suspension as if *Moondancer* was sailing through air, not water. And Christy would shrink down in the sleeping bag, covering her ears. Knowing by now what to expect.

And then would come the crash as they plunged down again into a solid wall of water, and the judder that ran through the little boat's planking as if it would tear her apart. And the awful bucking, tossing movement as the seas caught hold of her again, tossing her like a child's plaything in their inexorable grip.

If it weren't for the noise, she thought desperately, then I could bear the motion. But as it was, the two seemed to work together to pound her into a state of trembling, sickening fear. Nothing that she had ever felt before had prepared her for this complete mental and physical disintegration. It was an abject submission to terror that robbed her of her will.

And he was out there. . . Brand was out there in the storm. But she couldn't seem to take that in. No one could be out there, in that raging, rending fury of wind and water. He must have been swept overboard by now, or drowned where he stood at the wheel, in the waves that swept over the boat with such relentless force.

The nausea hit her again and Christy bent over the bucket. But her stomach was empty from the constant retching and she slumped back into the bunk, her head throbbing with the awful tightness that the sickness carried in its wake.

He must be dead. . . But somehow, as she floated in and out of consciousness, Christy knew that wasn't true. In her dreamlike state, she gradually became aware that she could feel his hand on the boat, as surely as if it had been on her own body. And the boat responded to him, as she had done. She could sense it. . .

She could feel him caress the wheel, coaxing *Moondancer* over or through the crests that towered green above them. And she could feel the wildness in the little boat's movements when he lost concentration and made a mistake. When that happened, she caught her breath, willing him on. And then the fight would continue.

In her half-sleep, Christy smiled. Outside, the storm raged just as fiercely. But she was no longer alone.

* * *

Christy couldn't have put her finger on the moment when she realised that the storm was beginning to abate. The wind and water still howled and crashed around her fragile world, buffeting her into a mindless, unthinking state of suspension. But somewhere inside her, it was as if a knot had begun to loosen. As if some deep instinct whispered that the worst was over. . .

At first, she hardly dared to believe it. But then she started to hear sounds which for hours had been drowned out by the savagery of the storm. The steady drub-drub of the engine. The crack of wind in the sails. And then, unmistakably, the sound of footsteps on the deck above her head. He was safe, then. . . And slowly, *Moondancer* stopped her wild plunging and steadied her gait.

Slowly and gradually, Christy's mind uncurled from the paralysis that had gripped it. The terror was almost over. She had survived. She was bruised and sick and cold and wet and frightened. But she was alive, and so was Brand.

Christy clambered out of the bunk to stand up free in the cabin, her legs shaking from the nausea and hours of confinement. And she became hazily aware of a feeling of *difference*; a sensation that, during the storm, something important had changed. Something she couldn't quite pin down. But something *significant*. . .

Painfully, stiffly, Christy shed her waterproofs and crept quietly up the steep ladder-like companion-way to the deck. And as she stuck her head out into the fresh, early morning air, she gasped with sheer delight.

The world was aflame; the sky behind and above the little yacht shot through with tongues of red and golden fire. And in the centre of it, on the horizon, the sun was rising out of the sea like a great orange ball.

Christy gazed at the spectacle entranced, all else forgotten, bound up in the unexpectedness of its beauty. It was a moment out of time; a glimpse of eternity. A promise of magic. . .

The golden transformation was short-lived. Within minutes, the splendour of the dawn was muted, fading to an all-suffusing glow as the great orb pursued its progress over the horizon, shrinking as it did so into just another daytime sun. But the memory of it was lodged somewhere inside her. It was a picture that she knew would never fade.

Half dazed, half dazzled by the sun, Christy looked around her, as if trying to remember where she was. And saw Brand.

He stood with utter stillness at the back of the boat. His oilskins lay discarded in a corner of the cockpit and his once immaculate dress-shirt was stained with sweat and open at the neck, exposing the skin and crisp dark hair beanth. His legs, still clad in the smooth black cloth of another world, were splayed for balance and his feet were bare as if to root him to the deck.

His eyes were dark with weariness. 'Christy.' One hand lay casually on the wheel, the tanned and roughened fingers as much a part of the boat as the use-worn surface of the wood itself. His face, silhouetted against the dying glory behind him, was in shadow. But she could feel his eyes.

And in an instant, she knew what that elusive sense of difference had really been, waking up in that little cabin where he must so often have slept. She was no longer afraid of him. And seeing his hand there on the wheel, steering with the almost imperceptible movements of a man in perfect harmony with his craft, she also knew why. And what she had to do.

'Brand.' His head tilted slightly, but he said nothing, and she still couldn't see the expression in his eyes.

'Brand——' The words were an effort to force out, their importance choking her and drying her mouth. What if it was too late? But she had to try. . . 'Brand, I'm sorry. I should have known—I did know, really. Somewhere inside. But I was so tired, I couldn't think.'

'What did you know?' The voice was calm and impersonal, as if they were discussing the weather. But behind the coolness of his façade, Christy could sense the tension with which he awaited her answer and it gave her hope.

'You didn't kill them, Brand. You're not a murderer.'

His hands had been telling her that; those strong, broad hands. The hands that had soothed her; caressed her. The hands that had held her safe, that had steered *Moondancer* safely through the night.

'However much you wanted Sutcliffe's back. However much you hated your brother and—and Melissa.'

She stumbled a little over the name, the thought of his grieving over another woman's loss biting with sudden jealousy. 'You wouldn't have sabotaged that helicopter—or had it done. I should have known that, whatever people said. Only why. . .?'

'Why didn't I tell you that?' Beneath the calm, his voice was raw with a bitterness that tore at her heart. 'Would you have believed me, Christy? From where I was standing, it seemed you'd drawn me into one of your neat little boxes and labelled it "murderer". Are you telling me that denying it would have done me any good?'

'I. . . I don't know,' Christy confessed. 'Perhaps not; not last night. I was. . .confused. But you might have given me the chance.'

'I did. I brought you here.' They both fell silent for a moment as the beauty of the scene pressed in on them. The sea was limpid and sparkling in the early morning light. 'It's the best remedy I know for confusion.'

Brand paused, his head alert as if to scent the freshening breeze, letting the wheel slip lightly under his hand until the sails cracked full and the boat reached the equilibrium he wanted.

'I loved Melissa,' he said at last, the words sounding as if they had been dragged out unwillingly from some deep, secret place. Christy felt her heart turn over with something like fear. She didn't want to hear this. But Brand's voice continued relentlessly, his eyes fixed on the horizon. And there was nothing she could do to stem the flow.

'Or at least, I thought I did. I wanted her badly, of course, and she was a clever woman as well as a beautiful one. She made it clear that it was marriage or nothing.' The bitterness in his words made Christy shiver. No wonder he had reacted so violently in the cave at Cheung Chow, when he had thought that she was playing the same game again. . .

But he was determined to go on. Christy could almost see the tension that locked his body. 'But I was young then, and I was a fool. I didn't see the obvious until it was staring me in the face.'

'What do you mean?' Her eyes were fixed on him now. She had to hear his story to the end.

'I mean that it was marriage to Sutcliffe Trading she wanted—not me. That was why she encouraged me to make my bid for control. But the odds I had to offer to get Joss to accept my gamble made my brother the favourite.'

Brand's voice hardened to stone. 'And Melissa wasn't prepared to settle for an outsider. So she decided to hedge her bets on the leader as well. My dear fiancée made sure Joss had every detail of my preparations for that race. And when I lost, she made her choice. When we sailed back into harbour, it was Joss she ran to meet. She walked past me as if I was a stranger.'

'Oh, Brand——'

He laughed shortly. 'If I'd got my hands round her neck then, I might have killed her. But I didn't. And the accident that happened was just that—an accident. Whatever anyone said.'

Christy wanted to go to him, but there was something unapproachable about his tall, dark figure. 'How did you bear it, the stories people were telling? Why didn't you deny them? Even Charlie. . .'

But as if a limit had been reached, he met her wide-eyed sympathy with a grin. 'Because it was good business, little rabbit. In Hong Kong, it does no harm to acquire a reputation for ruthlessness.'

His flippancy shocked her. 'What do you mean?'

'When I got back, after Joss was killed, I realised pretty quickly that if I was going to save Sutcliffe's I was going to have to use every weapon I could lay my hands on. Those rumours saved my face—and put me back on the map faster than anything else I could have devised. In fact, people were queuing up to do business with me.'

For a moment, the pirate mask shadowed his features, frightening her. Was there nothing he wouldn't do. . .? But then he flexed his arm, wincing at the stiffness, and the shadow was forgotten as she suddenly realised that he had been sailing right through the night. He must be so tired.

'I'm sorry, Brand.'

'Come here, Christy.'

He stood to one side, still controlling the wheel with the lightest of touches on the spokes, and beckoned her to him.

'Yesterday, I asked you to marry me——' he started. There was a note in his voice that Christy didn't recognise at first. But then she realised, with

shock, that it was diffidence. The supremely confident Brand Sutcliffe was unsure what to say.

'You didn't have to, Brand,' she said gently. 'You
still don't. I knew weeks ago that I would come to
you—on any terms. I just couldn't find the courage
until last night.'

He shook his head. 'And I couldn't find the courage to face what I was feeling, Christy. I must have
given you hell the past few weeks. I couldn't get you
out of my mind; I was obsessed with you. I wanted
you more than I'd ever wanted a woman. But I
couldn't admit that there might be more to it than
that.'

He smiled, wryly. 'Last night was a watershed for
both of us. When I saw you sitting there at the
computer—you were so beautiful, Christy, like an
animal on the edge of flight. I wanted to hold you,
and keep you. I suddenly felt I couldn't bear for you
to go.'

Christy realised she was holding her breath.

'I love you, little rabbit.' The words sent an electric
thrill of pleasure down her spine. 'I think I've loved
you since I first saw you in the airport, in that horrible
tracksuit, but I was too stubborn to admit it. After
Melissa, I swore I'd stick to casual relationships.'

'Like with Rainbow.' The words came out without
thinking. 'Oh, Brand—I'm sorry. I know it's none of
my business——'

'What are you talking about, little rabbit? Rainbow
is—or rather was, since I doubt if even she would
have the gall to turn up for work on Monday—my
secretary. She's never been anything else.'

Christy stared at him. 'But what about that night after the races? And the bracelet you gave her?'

'What?' Brand's tone of astonishment held the ring of truth. 'That evening was purely business, my jealous little rabbit—and very boring business too. Rainbow used to act as my hostess when I was entertaining, and I've had to do a lot of that these past few months. Hence the bracelet. I'd promised her a hefty bonus to make up for all the overtime and she asked for the bracelet instead of cash. One of my clients is a jeweller, so she knew I could get a good deal.'

He looked at Christy speculatively. 'So you thought I was keeping a mistress, did you? And you were prepared to condone it? How very Oriental of you. I must bear that in mind. . .'

'Don't you dare even think it, Brand Sutcliffe.' Christy could feel the laughter bubbling up inside her. 'It was only because I'd convinced myself that she was an *ex*-mistress. . . But in future, I'd be grateful if you could pay your secretaries by cheque. And save the presents for your wife.'

He looked at her as if not quite sure what he had heard. 'Christy. . . Am I going to have a wife?'

'So long as you promise not to drag me through any more typhoons. It's rather an eccentric form of courtship—even for a pirate.'

'That sounds fair enough.' His face darkened. 'I'm not proud of last night, Christy. Dragging you out in *Moondancer* with no radio and without checking the forecasts was criminally irresponsible. Can you really forgive me?'

'There's nothing to forgive. I learned something last night—something I should have realised a long time ago.' She looked down, too shy to meet his eyes. 'All this time, I've been judging you by my father, Brand. In some ways, you're very like him—you're a gambler by nature; you like taking risks. But that's as far as the similarity goes.'

At last she found the courage to look up. 'You're strong, Brand—I feel safe with you. Even last night, I felt safe. Poppa was always weak. The disasters were always someone else's fault. . . He could never have fought, the way you did last night——'

'I shouldn't have had to.' There was real pain in his voice. 'I could have killed you, Christy.'

'But you didn't, did you?' She smiled, remembering. 'You did what you set out to do. You taught me to live.'

'Ah, yes. The art of living dangerously. . .' Brand looked down at her with a love that was unmistakable and Christy moved closer, her body swaying gently with the motion of the boat. His free hand reached out to ruffle her hair and she leaned her face against it, almost unable to take in what he was saying to her. Marriage to Brand. . . It was like a dream come true.

But it wasn't a dream. It was the most real thing that had ever happened. . .

'It's going to be an exciting few years, Christy,' he whispered. 'Last night was closer than you knew; it could have gone either way until the last moment. But that's just the start of the battle. Now that I've got the backing, I'm going to fight to put Sutcliffe's where it belongs. And you can help me. We'll do it together.'

'Yes.'

Christy felt utterly at peace. Brand touched her face; and what had started as merely a gesture became a caress; his thumb moving in slow circles against the down of her cheek.

'Poor little rabbit,' he murmured. 'You've come a long way since that tracksuit, haven't you? You did disapprove of me so much. In fact, you were a very stubborn pupil.'

The steady circling continued, and Christy felt the delicate pleasure of it lulling her into an almost hypnotic trance.

'But we never got as far as the last lesson, did we, my love? I think you ought to finish the course. Or you might relapse.' His voice became softer still, so that she had to strain to pick out the words. And yet, looking into his eyes, she felt that even if she could have heard nothing at all, she would still have known exactly what he was saying.

The slow desire that he had awakened was burning in her like a fuse. And she knew only that she loved him. And wanted him. And that today, at last, her wanting would be assuaged.

'It's finally time for the last lesson, Christy. And we have all the time in the world.'

During the next few hours, Christy began to discover just how much sensual awareness could be packed into the most ordinary activities. Because despite the promise of his words Brand seemed to take a perverse pleasure in tantalising her; in keeping her almost—but not quite—at a distance.

He scarcely touched her. But the words they had spoken were still there, between them, and every second of accidental contact became suffused with awareness of what must inevitably follow.

Every touch set her skin and nerves on fire, burning the moments into her memory with an intensity that would never fade. . .

His hands covering hers as he stood behind her again at the wheel, showing her how to steer to the feel of the wind on her cheek, so that the sail filled tight and full and the little yacht danced through the waves, as lively as her name. . .

The warm roughness of his bare thigh against her hip, as they stood wedged together in the tiny galley, making sandwiches for lunch, while *Moondancer* rode lightly at anchor off the coast of a tiny islet which shone green as jade in the sunlight. . .

The wiry strength she felt in his arms as he pulled her dripping and laughing from the sea, in the silk camisole which was all she had to swim in.

And then, at last, the closeness as he took her, still wet and salty from her swim, into his arms. The intoxicating wave of desire that swept over her. And the burning in his eyes, and the hardness of his body against her, that told her he too was at the edges of his control.

For what seemed like hours, they just clung together, as if to move might break the spell. Then, without speaking, he drew her down on to the coarse

white canvas of a sail which lay on the deck. The
heat of the afternoon seemed to hang heavy around
them. Waiting.

'Christy.' The salt-caked folds of their makeshift
bed were rough against her back as he knelt over her
to cup her breasts, his thumbs teasing them through
the wet transparency of the silk. The damp fabric hid
nothing of her body's instant response. Christy felt
her heart quicken and a moisture flood her that had
nothing to do with the sea.

'Take it off, Christy.' Brand's voice was harsh with
a need that touched on desperation. 'I want to see
you.' She hesitated and saw him smile at her timidity.
'Don't worry, little rabbit. No one comes here; not
even the fishermen. This stretch of water is too rocky
for their nets. And there's nothing else to tempt
them. You're quite safe.'

'Am I?' The way it came out was both flirtation and
plea. 'Even from you?'

And then her eyes were caught and held by his,
and she felt her worries melt away. Slowly, her hands
went down to the thin silk straps and pulled them
down to expose her breasts to his lips. And she heard
the sharp hiss of his breath, and then his voice, low
and husky, answering her.

'Safe with me, Christy, but not from me. Never
from me.'

She would remember every second of what followed,
Christy knew, as if the liquid droplets of memory
had set into crystal, strung into a living necklace that

she could take and run through her hands. And with it, remember.

She would remember how he had knelt across her body, easing the wet silk gently from her buttocks and sliding it down her legs, then letting the flimsy garment fall damply to the ground.

How he had kissed her as if he would devour her with his hunger, burying his face in her belly, and between her breasts. How he had lain beside her as he slipped off his own shorts, and she had felt the touch of his flesh against her.

The feel of him was with her still; hard and yet soft as the petals of a flower; demanding yet strangely vulnerable; cool from the sea and yet heated from within with a fire that threatened to set her own body ablaze.

She would remember his urgency—and his gentleness, the agony of carefulness that twisted his face as he entered her. She would remember the ease of it, and her own surprise, and mounting pleasure. She would remember the slow, gentle movements, and the storm she felt building inside her.

She would remember the quickening. And to the end of her life she would remember his shout of exultation, as he carried them together over the edge.

Afterwards, they lay together, their bodies slick with sweat. Christy was silent, the jewels of memory more real than the world which surrounded them. Only the warmth of Brand's body beside her was real, and the rise and fall of his breath.

When he spoke, she was startled, as if in a world

of sensation and instinct, she had forgotten speech could exist.

'Happy, little one?'

'Mmm. . .' She rolled over on to her front, feeling with lazy delight the tremor that passed through him as her breasts brushed softly against his chest. 'You could say that. It would be terribly British and understated. But since we're in Hong Kong, I suppose I'd better admit that I'm in a state of delirious ecstasy.'

A slow smile spread over his face. 'You're getting the idea, Christy. That's what a man likes to hear.'

There was a thickness in his voice that reminded her how long it was since he had slept. His words vibrated through his chest and she ran her fingers thoughtfully through the damp curls of hair that lined its contours. Fascinated by the feel of it, she tugged gently at its crispness, revelling in the maleness of it, in the difference from her own skin.

'Brand, is it always like that?' she asked shyly. 'Or was it just beginner's luck?'

'No, my love.' He sounded oddly shaken. 'It isn't always like that. That was our own special magic.' He leaned up on one elbow, looking down at her as if in wonder. 'And as for beginner's luck. . .'

His words were definitely slurring now, and his eyelids drooping, the black lashes brushing his cheek. But as he leaned over her she could already feel his body stirring against her thigh.

'Next time, you won't be a beginner, Christy,' he murmured softly.

'Next time?' Her voice was gently teasing. 'I thought you were tired?'

'This time,' he growled. And pulled her towards him.

And as she lay nestled in the strong circle of his arms, Christy knew that this was all the refuge she ever needed.

She had found her safe harbour. And a captain to steer her through the storms.

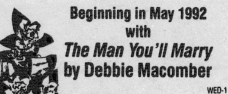

Following the success of **WITH THIS RING**,
Harlequin cordially invites you to enjoy the
romance of the wedding season with

BARBARA BRETTON
RITA CLAY ESTRADA
SANDRA JAMES
DEBBIE MACOMBER

A collection of romantic stories that celebrate the joy,
excitement, and mishaps of planning that special day
by these four award-winning Harlequin authors.

**Available in April at your favorite Harlequin
retail outlets.**